THE
SECOND GENERATION

BY

JAMES WEBER LINN

New York
THE MACMILLAN COMPANY
LONDON: MACMILLAN & CO., Ltd.
1902

Norwood Press
J. S. Cushing & Co. — Berwick & Smith
Norwood Mass. U.S.A.

To J. A.

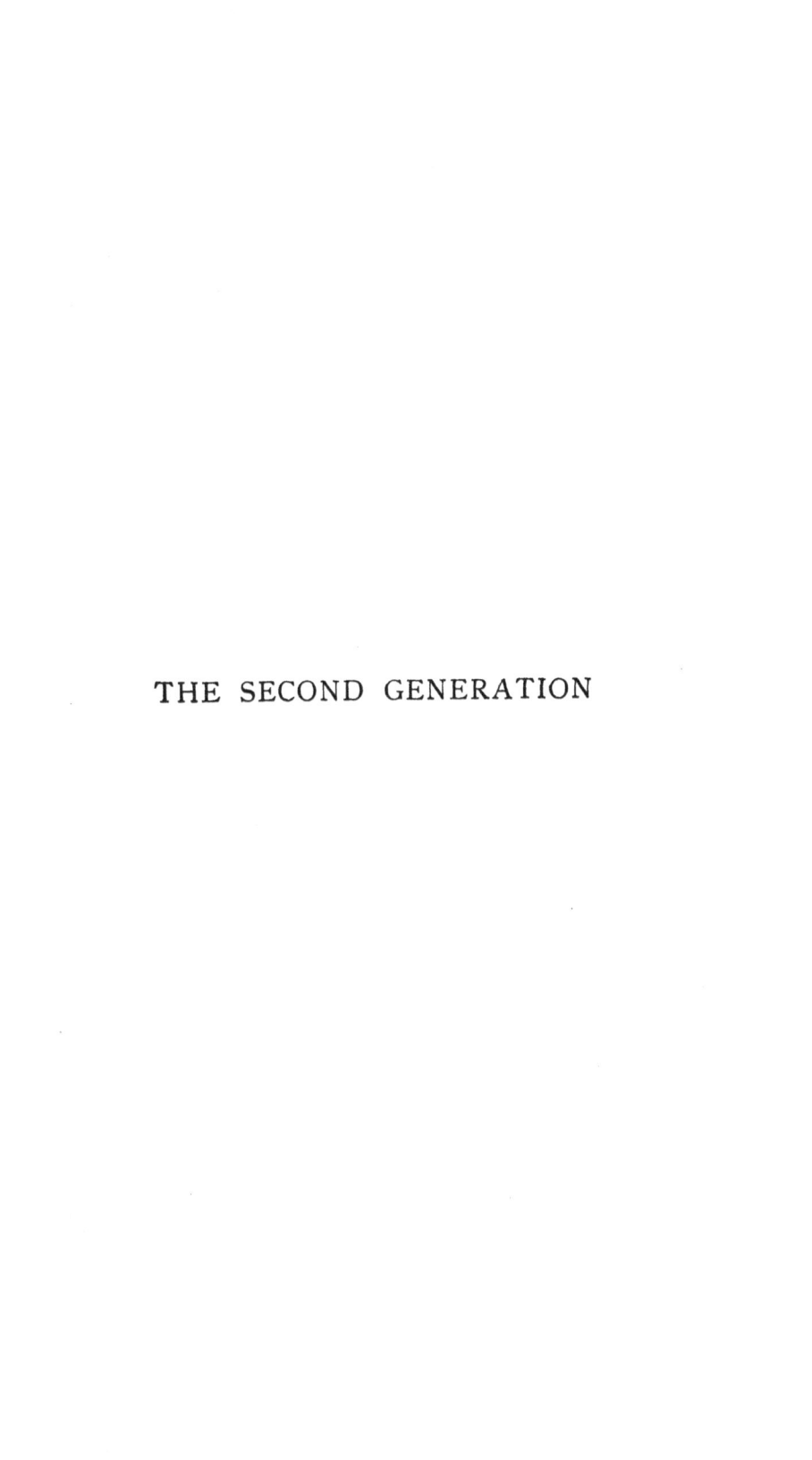

THE SECOND GENERATION

THE SECOND GENERATION

THE PROLOGUE

THE curtain rises on a stage as plain as the old Elizabethans',—a little bare room, containing a pine desk without a lid, three chairs, and two of the inevitable receptacles whose presence indicates, to the student of sociology, the habitat of the American politician, just as certain deep scratches on ancient petrified trees are said to be proof of the one-time presence, in those woods, of the megatherium. Maps covered the walls — maps wherein blue, red, yellow, and brown lines, striking an unerring course, were supposed to show the railroads of the state; maps cut into large and small squares, like trigonometrical paper, numbered, lettered, and shaded, to indicate the possessor of every forty acres of land in the county. A heavy odour of tobacco brooded over all. This room was the inner office of Christopher

Wheeler, generally known as the " boss of the 33d " — that is the 33d Congressional District of Indiana. The boss sat at his desk, dwarfing it. His physique was one great asset of his capital. His big red head flared like a torch on shoulders only less massive than the huge deformities of the Farnese Hercules; they squared themselves to bear it; in the evolution of that effort, Wheeler's neck, if he had ever had one, had long since disappeared. His great arms, the wrists thatched like an ape's with a close growth of hair, terminated in hands thick, stubby, and powerful as hammers. Those fingers could wrench a horseshoe into a flat bar, or tear a pack of cards across. As he leaned forward over the desk, to enforce his point, they thumped heavily among the papers. His clothes hung on him carelessly — a vast soiled shirt, crossed like a desert by the two pathways of his braces; trousers of good material, with a purple stripe. His shoes, even in Indiana, were perforce made to measure, a fact in which Wheeler took a possibly inordinate pride.

At the moment his face was crinkled into a wide and ingratiating smile. But John Kent was not to be appeased by a smile. The Editor of the *Scannell County Clarion,* lank, dark-faced, with a thin neck thrust above a low collar and a loose string tie, restless, bright, wide-set eyes, small ears, wide mouth close-shut, looked like those lithographs of Henry Clay which you may see on the lid of certain boxes of cigars. His long, thin fingers were stained with ink, and his stained cuffs above them were frayed and careless. In a drawing-room he would have made a poorer figure than the boss, perhaps.

" See here, Chris," he insisted, " I don't say you *want* to dodge, but it looks to me as if you were dodging just the same. I promised the boys you'd give a straight answer to a straight question, and it's going to hurt you if you don't. Are you, or ain't you, going to vote for the Consolidated? "

Wheeler's smile slowly gave way to a look of deliberation; his eyes met Kent's squarely. " Well, John," he answered, " 's far's I can see now, I reckon I am."

The little Editor had more than half expected it; yet it startled him when it came.

At this time, and especially in that part of

Indiana nearly surrounding Scannell County, the first burst of the discovery of oil had passed, and the country was engaged in developing its resources in a systematic, if somewhat scattered, manner. Hundreds of small firms were embarked in the oil business, buying, refining, shipping — on a small scale but with steady profits. Into this hive of industry came a huge stone — the announcement that the Consolidated Oil Company not only sought a charter to do business in the state, but were on the point of securing one. The governor was understood to be favourable to their project; only the individual legislators, then, stood between the company and its aims. Many of these, especially from districts where no trace of oil could be detected, had seen no reason why the development of the business should not fall altogether into the hands of one company; but for two years the majority had stood the other way. Now for the third time the bills chartering the company had been introduced, and the opposition to it was said to be much less steady. Rumours of fabulous sums offered here and there by the lobbyists of the company began to have a double effect: they

roused the small firms to terror, and excited
the cupidity of even the most honest. Honest
and dishonest, however, among the congress-
men of the oil districts, stood together for a
time against the innovation, the one in the fear
of God, the others of their constituents. Suddenly the news crept abroad somehow that
Chris Wheeler, politically as physically the
biggest man in that part of the state, would
vote for the coming of the Consolidated; Chris
Wheeler, whom the men of the oil district had
put and kept in power, till their united support,
always ready to hand, made his reëlections
matters of course. The rumour was laughed at
for two days. Then when no savage denial was
issued by Wheeler, it was laughed at no more.
They wrote him, some angrily, some appeal-
ingly, some apparently half-amused. For re-
sult he left the legislature for a day, and came
home to answer for his deeds. When they
heard he was in town, his constituents breathed
more freely, for it was argued that he would
never dare face them if he intended to tell them
they were betrayed. Some few, Kent among
them, who knew with more exactitude the
character of their representative in the state

legislature, were not even then quite assured. This view was expressed, briefly, by one Theophilus Green, known as "File," by avocation fisherman and woodsawyer, by vocation political philosopher and prophet.

"Chris Wheeler," he remarked, "ain't afraid of nothin' but bein' poor. And ef it's true he's goin' to vote for the Consolidated, I reckon he ain't afraid of *thet,* no more." Having personally nothing at stake in the matter in question, File, as usual with disinterested Americans, affected the cynically-amused. But the major part of the delegation which, unofficial but serious, wended toward Wheeler's office the next morning, went to have its temporary gloom dispelled. Wheeler was there before them; greeted the first of them cordially; then withdrew with Kent, the principal spokesman of the crowd, to his inner office. This move reawoke the sleeping fears. Why should he not disclaim publicly among them any intention of supporting the dreaded company? So they alternated in confidence and trepidation, wandering into the passage to spit, and back again to discuss and wonder, till gradually the outer office and the hallway were nearly filled with uneasy voters, shepherd dogs, and a few boys anxious for excitement. But still the conference within went on.

The little Editor was startled indeed. If Chris Wheeler, for whatever reason, should announce a determination to support the Consolidated Company, a host of wavering legislators would fall in behind him. The whole plan was clear as sunlight. Given a strong man who could be induced to bear responsibility and odium: the rest was easy. Kent wondered rapidly how much the inducement had been. What could he say to offset greed? He had known Wheeler for years; should he try appeal?

"Chris," he said directly, "you're not in earnest?"

The big man's face hardened. "Why not, then?"

"You can't afford it, Chris. Why, every man in the district would be down on you. Look at the crowd out there now. You know what they think; you're the only man between them and ruin. They've put you there; what'll they say if you turn against 'em? what'll they do?"

Wheeler shifted his big bulk. "Do? they'll come round, John. Some of 'em don't see this thing in quite the right way. They're good people, but they're narrow. When the Consolidated has been in Indiana a year, they'll be coming up here in droves to thank me."

"I wonder if Tom Bayard will come up too," remarked Kent, meditatively. "I was down to Medora last Saturday, and I had dinner with him. He's got a nice little wife and two little children. 'How's business?' said I. 'Fine; just waking up,' he says. But he looked a little worried. 'What's the matter, Tom?' I asked him.

"'Well,' he said, 'it's this d——d Consolidated Company. People keep on chattering and chattering, how it's bound to get in here. 'F it does, it's all day with me; they'll undersell me, steal all my business, and drive me right out. I had to starve the missis awhile just after we were married, and I kind of hate to think of doing it again. That's the hell of having kids,' he said, 'it makes you nervous.' I tried to cheer him up. 'Here's Chris,' I told him, 'the old red-headed rock of Gibraltar, he'll never let the Consolidated people ride over

us little fellows; he's a match for them.
What'd you help elect him for?' It seemed to
kind of refresh him. 'That's so,' he said. 'I
reckon it's safe enough!' D'you think he'll
come up with the rest of them to thank you,
Chris?"

The big boss stirred uneasily again. As he
had gone over the matter in his mind, he had
made an abstract question of it. It was a
problem of dollars and cents, of the ultimate
development of business and resources. Suddenly, out from among the figures, here leaped
a man, an actual man he knew, Tom Bayard of
Medora, who might be forced to starve his wife
and children. But the impression was only
momentary; Political Economy came rapidly
to his relief.

"See here, John," he explained, "if the Consolidated is going to bust Tom Bayard or anybody else — mind I don't admit that it is, but
if it is — how can I help it? I was elected to
do the best I could for the state of Indiana.
She's got oil; she needs money. These two-
cent firms can't help her out. What she wants
is a company with capital, that can use all the
latest methods in producin' and sellin' both, a

company that moves by machinery from start to finish. That's what she wants, and that she's got to have, if it kicks over every little private derrick from here to h——l. Why, 'f I didn't know that in two years you'll see it as I do, d'you think I'd run the risk of supporting this company? You've said yourself they'll all go back on me; it'll be ' Chris the robber ' — I can hear 'em. But let 'em talk, John, let 'em talk; let 'em throw me over next election and pick up some fool that goes with the crowd. They'll find out fast enough he *is* a fool, and back they'll come a-running to get a man again. I'm not Tom Jefferson nor Andrew Jackson, but I can see through a hole anyway. They can retire me; they can scrape the butter off my bread, and be d——d to 'em; but when I see a thing is the right thing, right for me, right for the state, right for everybody, why — " He picked up an enormous handkerchief from the desk, and mopped his face and neck, heated by his own oratory.

" How much are they giving you, Chris? " said Kent, in the tones of one asking for a match.

As the meaning of the question penetrated

Wheeler's brain his face became hideous; the thick lips seemed to draw back like a dog's; tremendous molars, stained yellowish brown by tobacco, started into view; the great nose and the eyes drew closer together; and just as at the end of his previous speech, Wheeler had seemed powerful and almost manly, he looked now one instant later powerful and almost devilish.

" How's that? " he demanded, heavily.

" How much are they giving you, Chris? "

" You — you — "   Wheeler paused, it seemed because the swelling veins in his neck were choking him. " Get out of here," he cried fiercely, when for a moment the two men had stared at each other in silence. He rose with the words. But Kent held his ground.

" You talk about the state of Indiana," he pursued rapidly. " Why, if you saw a man with one hand on her throat and the other grabbing her pocket-book, would you make a speech or would you jump in and pull him off? I reckon it would depend on how much was in the pocket-book. Why, Chris Wheeler, I've known you fifteen years and more; do you think you can fool me with your talk about the development of resources? I asked you how much you would get, didn't I? Well, it's what every man, woman, and child in the 33d District will ask with me. It's what the *Scannell County Clarion* will ask at the head of every column till I'm under ground or you are. You work for the Consolidated Oil Company, and you're a dead coon, Chris Wheeler — deader'n mackerel. You can't get another vote out of the 33d with a pickaxe. Well, what do you think? Are these principles of yours worth it? Think about it, Chris; think about it a long time." Kent's sneer was unconcealed; he had dropped his mask of calmness. He stood alert, expecting nothing else than physical violence on the part of Wheeler. But the boss had to some degree regained control over himself. He confined himself to abuse.

" You think so? Who are you, you half-fed ink-slinger? Where have you got to in the world — proprietor of a dirty little Scannell County, patent inside, job-printing, hand-press weekly, a man that can't buy soap and meat the same week! You talk about principles?" He pulled a silver dollar from his pocket, with one twist of his powerful fingers bent it double,

and tossed it in a corner. " Principles? By
G——d, if I left this office you'd go snooping
over there for the money ! "

" I shouldn't wonder if every dollar you
owned was as crooked as that one," remarked
Kent. No sooner had he spoken than with a
backhanded slap Wheeler knocked him down.
For a moment he lay still while the politician,
still enraged, stood over him; then he rose
painfully and went out, like a man dazed.

As he appeared, holding a handkerchief to
his bleeding face, white as death under the
blood and tan, a chorus of exclamations greeted
him. He held up his hand and there was
silence.

" Our representative," he said, " has decided to vote for the Consolidated Oil Company's bill."   Then, disregarding questions
and exclamations, leaving tumult and wonderment behind him, he passed out into the street.
The hot May sun poured unheeded on his bare
head.   He saw no one, heard nothing but
Wheeler's voice ringing in his ears. From moment to moment, mechanically, he put up his
handkerchief afresh to stanch the blood dripping slowly from his nostrils. Sometimes he

leaned against the fence for support. Once, making a misstep, he fell; but again picked himself up and plodded on. To the casual observer, if there had been any such, he must have seemed very drunk. At length he reached his own house, entered it, and lay down upon a couch. His wife, coming singing into the room by chance some minutes later, found him there, his clothes dusty from his fall, his face covered with dirt and blood, a bubble of foam between his discoloured lips. She thought him dead, and the song ended in a scream, but the sound of her voice seemed to call his faculties back. He opened his eyes.

" Where's Jerome? " he asked thickly.

" Jerome? " she repeated wildly.

" Call the boy," he repeated. " I want him."

She groped weakly about the room with her eyes; she believed him crazy, delirious. But at this moment a young boy of seven or eight, carrying a long whip, made his appearance in the doorway.

" Ged up! " he cried, lashing the legs of a chair; then, perceiving his father, an unwonted presence at that hour, he ran over to him.

"Oh, Pop," he demanded, "what are you doing here? Come and play horses." Suddenly the spectacle of dust and blood robbed him of speech, and he stood with mouth open, wondering. Kent began to speak with effort, and partly it seemed to himself.

"I told him the truth, Mame, and then he hit me."

"He has killed you," she moaned.

Kent made a feeble motion of dissent. "No, no, it's my heart, the old trouble. It was the excitement, not the blow; he didn't hurt me, Mame. I'll be — all right — soon." He waited a space, collecting his energies again, with closed eyes. Suddenly the words shot from him in a torrent. "No, no, no, it's not for myself I mind. But I must fight him to the end, Mame. He's a liar and a thief; he's going to ruin all his friends. He'll not stay in Kirksville; he can't. But I must follow him wherever he goes; I must show every one what he is; he must get no more friends to betray like these. Never, never, never! Jerome!"

The boy drew near, hesitating, reluctant.

"We must help each other, boy. Will you help papa?"

"John!" cried his wife. "What are you saying?"

"Yes, yes," he insisted weakly but doggedly; and he put out a hand until he had clasped his child's. "Not revenge, Mame; only justice. I don't want revenge; I provoked him. But he must do no more harm that I can help. I may go any time; then Jerome must take my place and fight my fight."

Jerome's mother with one swift motion caught the child away. "A baby — to say such things to a baby," she protested with a sob.

"He will grow up." Again the little Editor sank back exhausted. His wife, frightened and not knowing what else to do, brought a basin of water and timidly bathed his face. Then, the child assisting, she got him into bed, and — since he would not have her bring a doctor — set about preparing various homely remedies. Meanwhile a delegation of farmers came to consult with the Editor about Wheeler's action; but she told them he was ill, and they went slowly away. When Kent heard that they had come and gone he would have risen to follow them in spite of her tears, but he lacked the strength. So, lying still, he cried softly like a punished child.

"Oh, you shouldn't have done that, you shouldn't have done that, Mame," he repeated. "I might have helped them someway!"

CHAPTER I

Among the crowd pouring from the Polk Street railroad station in the city of Chicago walked a young man, leisurely looking about him. The May sun greeted him like an old friend, lighting up with appreciation his broad shoulders and fine head, and seeming to smile at his clothes of a country cut. He smiled back, except when some odour, unusually pronounced, smote his nostrils, when he sniffed suspiciously.

"Not exactly apple blossoms either," he murmured to himself, thinking of the forests of bloom that he had left behind. "Well, well!" He brought up with a round turn before a grimy window filled with revolvers, brilliants, accordions, boxing-gloves, and other débris left there by the ebbing tide of fortune, and stared with interest at the collection. "That must be a pawnshop, eh?" He looked upward. "If it is, there ought to be three gilt balls," he thought; and a satisfied smile in a moment lay upon his lips. There were.

Then he sauntered on up Clark Street, continuing to survey the place in which he had come to live. All his preconceived ideas of great cities he had from books. This was his first bit of actual experience. To one interested in Chicago it seems a pity that on leaving the stations of almost all the railroads the stranger must plunge at once into some of the most sordid and unpleasant quarters of the town. First impressions are proverbially difficult to remove. Jerome Kent read newspapers as well as books, and the newspapers of Chicago are most indefatigable heralds of the city's filth as well as of its magnitude; yet the reality came to the countryman with an unpleasant shock.

"These roads," he meditated, glancing at the shaky and splintering wooden blocks that served for pavement, "are just about as bad as ours in Scannell County; and yet here there is more traffic in an hour than we have in a year." He noticed that the liquor trade was prominently represented on both sides of the street. "Saloons, and a few shops," was his summary. A tin box at a corner, wide-mouthed, tottering

on three legs, caught his eye. It had been red
at one time, but the original colour was now
doubly overlaid with advertisements and dirt.
A legend ran across the top, confused among
the grimy praises of newspapers, drugs, and
biscuits. Jerome stooped to read it: —

"Help keep the city clean."

He looked about him, — at low-browed and
filthy doorways, at the wavering and filthy
pavement, down the long perspective of gray
and garish fronts, and upward at the well-
meaning sun in an obscured and smoky sky.
Then he laughed. This box, with the pitiful
motto, was a confession. "Poor devils," he
said aloud, "they need help." In all the view
there was not one point to hold and relieve the
eye, not one indication of any desire above a
beast's.

He had come to Jackson Boulevard, wondering. Now it unrolled its dark gray ribbon
before him, shining between grim and perpen-
dicular walls of masonry, carried up like forts
into the clouds. It was a street level and
straight. Carriages passed up and down, bicy-
cles slid in and out like spindles through a web.
The tunk-a-tunk, tunk-a-tunk-tunk of horses'

hoofs rang in his ears. Straining his eyes, he fancied that far down lakeward he could catch a glimpse of blue. It was part of a city, this, a city busy and commercial, a city with little time over for pleasure and the cultivation of the soul and mind, but a city of civilization and not of civic savagery, such as that other street belonged to and foretold. He swung his glance down that once more. A tramp, bristly and tattered, jostled him. Down a little way a saloon door opened suddenly, and with involuntary quickness and an expression of sodden despair another wayfarer appeared and fell in a heap on the sidewalk. He lay there, cursing; nobody heeded him. Jerome wondered again. Was this the past and present; or were both streets present, and would both be future?

After some search he discovered the office of the *Eagle*. It towered conspicuously enough even among the masses of steel and stone about it, ten stories, like a cliff. When he reached the elevator, he meant to time the ascent; but the noiseless cage whirled him up halfway before he could get out his watch. Mr. Northrop's office was No. 916, the negro operator informed him, the third door on the left,

Then the negro and his machine fell again into
their cavern, and Jerome found himself waiting for the interview he had so long anticipated.

He had time, however, to pull himself together before the attendant allowed him to
enter Northrop's private office. He had time
to notice all the details of the panelled waiting
room; the red walls, the black and upholstered
chairs, the string of tiny gold beads, infinitesimal electric lights, that ran about the moulding.
He had time to wonder whether all business
men in Chicago thus received all applicants in
sybaritic luxury, above a surging panorama
of roofs and swaying smoke — and what his
own chance was to be; whether this tremendous congeries of smoke and iron and stone
and flesh and blood, roaring now about and
below him, would ever know that he had come
into it in the flush of his youth, or would swal-
low him up as it had swallowed a million
others, and leave him to die, finally, and his
name, erased from the directory, to be cut on a
tombstone, and nobody a particle the wiser.
What were the qualities of success, he demanded of himself, or was it largely chance?

His father and this man Northrop, whom he was about to see, provided the big negro consented to hand in his name — they had been together at their little college in southern Indiana. His father, he had been told, was the stronger student of the two; when, out of college, for the first time the friends met in competition — over a girl — again it was his father who had won. The disappointment had driven young Northrop to the city on the lake. Now he was rich; he was married too, Jerome knew, so that even the long ago trouble was smoothed out of his mind. Suppose his mother, Jerome wondered, had chosen Northrop instead of Kent; would Kent be here, in that case, known of all men; would it be Northrop who would be sleeping down there in Indiana, under ground or above, it mattered little? The automatic Ethiopian cut across his meditations; Jerome awoke to be ushered into the private room of the owner of the *Eagle*.

Northrop rose to meet him and shook hands cordially.

"So this is John Kent's son." He put a thin hand on Jerome's shoulder. "You're far bigger than your father was. Well, well! Do you remember him?"

"Pretty well, sir," Jerome answered. "I was nearly eight when he died."

"And now?"

"I am twenty-five."

"Twenty-five! Don't say the words to me, my boy; you make me envious. To think of being twenty-five! Well — I have your mother's letter here, and the one you wrote me a few days ago to say you were coming. I am glad to see you come. Have you had luncheon? Come along with me." He rang sharply, two or three times, although the echo of the first sound had scarcely died away before the attendant answered.

"Robert, my coat." The negro produced a heavy garment; thinking of the sun without, Jerome stared. But Northrop wrapped his frail body in its folds with satisfaction. He was a small man, white-haired, bloodless apparently; he seemed the incarnation of the adjective *delicate*. Blue veins lay in tracery upon his hands and forehead and even his eyelids. When they went out, two or three people were still waiting; a woman half rose.

"I shall be back at three, Robert."

"But Mr. Northrop — " she began.

"I can't see you now, no, not now," he returned irritably. "Well, well — what is it, if you please? Just a moment, Kent." He conferred with her in low tones. "Yes, yes," he said finally. "Very worthy object, I see. I shall send you a check this afternoon. Pardon my rudeness; I am very tired." He smiled faintly.

When they were in the carriage, Northrop leaned back wearily and closed his eyes. "I have been seeing Tom, Dick, and Ella—mostly Ella — this morning for three hours," he apologized. "I shouldn't want you to think me rude. But these good women are so persistent! You can handle a man; but a good woman — what can you do but listen to her?" They rattled over the cobbles, Northrop's delicate, tired face very small indeed, muffled in his overcoat and cap. When the carriage stopped he opened his eyes once more.

"The Athletic Club," he murmured. "I half hoped it would be that to-day. I generally let Julius — Julius is my coachman — choose the place for my luncheon. The food is equally bad everywhere."

"Now," he said, when they were seated, "suppose you tell me all about it."

" About it ? "

" About your plans, I mean; what you would like to do. You spoke in your letter of going to work on the *Eagle;* are you still of that mind ? "

" You know," answered Jerome, " I have been a printer all my life. I shouldn't care to throw my experience away."

Northrop nodded. " But a weekly in the country and a daily in the city are two very different matters — as different as diamond and coal; as different as a book and a machine. The country paper, rightly ordered, is a personality; the daily is only a business. Do you think I write for the *Eagle?* I never write a line. The paper is mine, because I oversee it, but it is only a business enterprise. There is nothing of *me* in it."

" But if I worked on it," began Jerome.

The old man interrupted. " Would you set type? You would have to forget all your old methods and learn the ways of a machine. Or do you want to be a clerk? I have a hundred who never write a line for publication; I doubt if many of them read the paper they are working for. Out of all the employees of the *Eagle,*

how many do you suppose ever see their words
in print? Two-thirds? Half? A quarter? I
believe a tenth would be nearer — the reporters
and some of the editors."

"It was as a reporter I meant to begin."

"But what experience have you had there?
I tell you the work is wholly different. You
must turn your nights into days, of course;
that you probably know. But do you know
that you must become conscienceless, unscrupulous as a detective? The paper must have the
news, or the public will cease to read it. Therefore you must supply news; by fair and honest
means when you can, by every means in your
power sometimes. You must violate privacy
and confidence, deny yourself the luxury of
friends, forget your own soul and body. A
reporter works in an intellectual sweatshop.
What experience have you had to help you in
that? You don't even know the names of the
streets. Were you brought up to be honest
and to tell the truth? You will not find reporting a help in either."

Jerome looked blank. "But why —" He
stopped.

"Why do I employ young men to do such

things? That was to be your question, eh?
I must, if the paper is to succeed. I think the
paper is a good one and an honest one on the
whole. Besides, if I give it up, I should have
no grip anywhere. I like many things, I dislike many others. How could I praise one and
fight the other, without my paper to help me?
But I don't reason about it. I love it." He
laughed, and Jerome, glad of the opportunity,
laughed also.

"Tell me," demanded Northrop, abruptly,
"how did you leave Indiana? Were the horse-
chestnuts out? Could you smell the hawthorn?"

"You know the bend, where the road turns
to cross Skinner's Run, just south of town?"

Northrop shook his head. "No. I have
forgotten all my geography. But I can smell
the hawthorn still. Is there any left?"

"I walked out there yesterday," Jerome af-
firmed. "The side of the road was white with
it. I haven't seen so much for a long time."

"You care for it, then? My wife doesn't
like it; she won't let me have it in the house.
But sometimes I get to thinking of it, and the
fragrance comes back so strongly I have to get

up and look round; I think she has put some in
my room to surprise me. But I can never find
it. How long since you strolled along in the
dark, when the world was all black, and suddenly ran upon the fragrance of a bush of it?"

"Three days ago," answered Jerome.

"I haven't done that these ten years," Northrop returned regretfully.

When the waiter had brought their cigars,
Northrop settled back further into his chair.

"I have been doing the talking while you
listened," he said. "Now suppose you tell me
something about yourself — no more than you
care, of course. Don't think I'm trying to
force your confidence. But we must be friends,
you and I. How long since your mother died,
Jerome?"

"Two months, sir. It came very suddenly
after she wrote you. Your letter — she showed
it to me. It helped her very much, she said."

Northrop stirred uneasily. It embarrassed
him to be caught in kindness. "Nothing,
nothing," he muttered. "Go on, my boy."

"Well, sir, that's about all. She died, and
as soon as I could sell off the paper I came up
here."

" Did it sell well? "

" Fairly. But it was mortgaged, of course; and that took most."

" Have you any money? "

" Plenty, sir," answered Jerome, flushing. He had one hundred and twenty-five dollars — and his trunk.

Northrop eyed him.

" You saw the letter I wrote to your mother? I said I would see that you had what I could give you. Don't you think I meant it? "

" I am sure you did, Mr. Northrop," replied Jerome, very much embarrassed.

" Yet you resent my questions — don't you? Well, never mind. Had your mother ever spoken of me before she wrote? " he added abruptly.

" Often; yes, sir."

" What did she say? "

Jerome flushed again. He was torn between pride and a desire to pour himself out to some one. Should he put himself on guard, try to parry these downright thrusts; or should he meet Northrop's blunt questions with a blunt confidence? He thought himself a fool for hesitating. He had never in his life, he thought, met a more kind-hearted man than this frail, white-haired, curious old gentleman, who decried his own business and grew wistful over a roadside flower. But Jerome's nature was stiff, hard to bend. Sometimes he found himself unwilling — no, unable is the better word — to do or say what he longed and thought wise to do or say. So now. He remained tongue-tied, longing to open his heart, the words ready to his lips, but dammed, it seemed, unalterably. More and more as she grew older, his mother had spoken of Northrop, rising like a star on their horizon. She had had none of Jerome's reticence and unease. She told him everything — the story of his father's success and Northrop's failure in the struggle for her hand. If now and then, amidst all her loyalty to her dead husband, the least note of regret for the wide life she had missed when she made her choice long ago crept into her voice, was it unnatural? But the boy, passionately devoted in spirit to that ever young father whose death he remembered clearly, heard the note whenever it appeared; and since, loving his mother too, he might not turn his resentment upon her, he had been used to fasten it upon the unconscious Northrop. It was this childish feeling that now rose up at Northrop's question — a feeling to be smiled at, but yet not easily perhaps to be smiled down. While they sat, conscious each of their failure to meet in complete accord, a man strolled over from another part of the room. Northrop introduced Jerome to Judge Hetheridge.

"How's the merry war, Henry?" Hetheridge demanded. He was a bulky man, white-haired like Northrop, but with a red face and twinkling eyes. "I'm so busy nowadays I can't read your magazine, Henry; I only have time for the newspapers. But I hear you're up to your old tricks, fighting right and left all proposals for a steady government. It's the gas bill now, they say. There's too much gas about the *Eagle* altogether, Henry." He laughed heartily.

"It's lazy men like you, Judge, that make me do all the fighting. If you would only live up to your principles now, I might drop back and rest awhile."

"My only principle," returned Hetheridge, "is to avoid a row on my own account. The

D

good God knows I see enough of other people's
to teach me the wisdom of quietness. But you
are a ' scrapper,' Henry; you can't rest unless
your club is banging somebody, the bigger the
better. Who is getting it now — it's Wheeler
again, hey?"

"Yes," answered Northrop, with a sudden
return to weariness. "Wheeler again. Judge,
if you can only get that man comfortably in-
dicted, and remove him safely to Joliet, I will
promise you to make the *Eagle* a dove — until
he gets out again."

"Indict him? On what charge, for choice?"
questioned Hetheridge, comfortably. "Shall
we make it murder, or arson, or assault and
battery on the feelings of one Henry Northrop?"

"Any charge, any charge," said Northrop,
irritably. "If I could only get hold of the
facts in this gas-bill business we would make
it bribery."

"Ah, Henry," the Judge answered, getting
up, "if you talk to me like that, it is my duty
not to listen. Besides, my cigar is smoked out.
Come and see me, young man. But don't
come in the way of business." He chuckled

as he shook hands. " You understand? I shall deem it very unfortunate if I see you in business hours."

" One of the judges of the criminal court," explained Northrop.

" You were speaking of Wheeler," remarked Jerome, glad of the interruption. " Is that Christopher Wheeler, the banker? "

" Banker, manipulator, politician — everything but honest man," supplemented Northrop. " Yes, that is Chris Wheeler. An Indiana man like ourselves — did you know that? "

Jerome drew a long breath. " It was partly on his account that I came to Chicago," he confessed.

Northrop darted a look at him so keen, so sudden, that Jerome instinctively drew back as from a blow. " What has Wheeler to do with you? " he demanded.

" It is a long story," answered Jerome. " Did you ever hear how my father died? "

Northrop reflected. " Heart disease, wasn't it? "

" Yes, sir. But do you know what brought on the final collapse? "

Again there was a pause, while Northrop's eyes turned inward. "No, I never knew."

"It was a blow."

"A blow?"

"Yes, sir. From Wheeler's fist."

The other bounded in his chair. The frowning scrutiny which had followed Jerome's introduction of the name gave place to complete, blank surprise. "Wheeler's?" he gasped.

"Yes, sir."

"But — how?"

"They quarrelled over a political matter. Wheeler was instrumental in getting through a bill to charter the Consolidated Oil Company, which was just then entering the field. He had been elected to keep it out of Indiana if he could. My father charged him with dishonesty, and Wheeler knocked him down. My father never got over the shock. He died in six months."

"And Wheeler was not arrested?"

"No, sir. My father would never allow it. He had curious ideas sometimes, I believe. And after he died — there were no witnesses. Of course people talked. But Wheeler had moved to Chicago three months before my father's death. You see the Consolidated Oil Company ruined a good many people, and he could hardly stay in Scannell County very comfortably. Indeed, I suppose he would hardly have been safe there, especially after my father died."

" Well, sir ? "

Jerome coloured. " It will seem very odd to you, I know," he admitted. " But — will you look at that, Mr. Northrop? " He drew from an inner pocket an old-fashioned, yellow leather case, of the sort which in some parts of the United States is called a wallet; extracted a folded paper, yellowish also, and very worn; and handed it to Northrop. Opening it, the editor saw lines of faded writing, and down below a scrawling signature. He peered at it, fumbled for his eye-glasses, then handed it back. " Read it, please." Jerome read.

" ' I promise in the sight of God and man to devote my life to this one thing. I will see that Christopher Wheeler does as little harm in the world as possible.' That is my signature at the end," he went on. " I was nearly eight years old."

"And now?"

"It was eighteen years ago."

"That is a curious document though. In your father's writing, isn't it? Poor John! And you," he turned quickly, "what have you done?"

Jerome coloured again. "Nothing."

"Nothing!"

"What could I do?" Jerome demanded in self-defence. "We were poor; I could never, even when I grew older, leave my mother. And besides, she was always opposed even to my keeping this. It was the only thing I did habitually that was contrary to her wishes. She wanted me to destroy it, to forget it. She thought sometimes that my father was — not quite right in his head when he died. Maybe — she may have been right. She thought opposing Wheeler became a monomania with my father in those last six months."

"It may well be," Northrop muttered. "Sometimes I think it has become so with me. By G——d," he added, with a rare profanity, "it shall be now! You know," he went on, "what Wheeler is up to at present?"

"I thought he was out of politics," Jerome said.

" So he is — in a way. He only stirs up the slime from the bank, now. In another way he *is* politics. To-day he is engaged in putting through a bill to allow the government of each city of 100,000 population in the state to deal individually with all questions of franchise for corporations. He is very heavily interested in gas, here in Chicago. The franchises of the present company will expire in two years. If he can get his bill through, it means millions to him — millions! for he can easily bribe the council to give him his own terms of continuance. If the bill fails, he is still a very rich man, but he will be hard hit. It will be difficult for him to make good terms of sale for his company, impossible to extend the franchise. He will meet competition on all sides. So you understand — that he finds it essential to secure the passage of his bill." Northrop's finely veined lids drew together. "*I* find it essential to prevent him. It is our one chance. If we can beat him off here, we may force him to let the city alone, to retire on what he has stolen so far. If not — there is no hope for us. He will domineer to the end; he will suck us dry."

" He is so strong, then?"

Northrop nodded. " He — or circum-stances. Sometimes I wonder whether luck has not always been with him. I have hopes of its turning, you see. Indeed, I have strong hopes that we shall prevent the passage of this bill. But that will not satisfy me. I should like to prove him a felon. If I could only get evidence! Every one knows he bribes. But it is impossible to convict a man of bribery, in America. They want evidence, evidence. Bah! When I smell assafœtida, I don't need to see the body to know that a skunk has been there. So you have come up here to fight Wheeler," he ended.

Jerome smiled. " It's a big contract, isn't it? And besides — sometimes — " He paused. " Mr. Northrop, the Consolidated Oil Company has been a very good thing for the state of Indiana."

" Pooh, pooh!" answered Northrop, angrily.

" Yes, sir. It has brought our part of the state up with a run. They see it, even down there, now. Wheeler is still a tradition of evil, but they admit, sometimes, that he was right when he told them it would help the

state. Is it possible that he saw farther than
my father? I have noticed that a number of
the bills he has been interested in have turned
out well. What do you think?"

"No fault of his," snapped the old man.
"But yes — you are right. He has had wonderful luck; and he plumes himself upon it.
But it is the way he secures his ends that dis-
gusts me. Always evil; at best they are evil
that good may come; at the worst, they are
unpardonably devilish. Corruption and bribery, bribery and corruption, follow him always.
So you don't want to fight him?"

"Yes, sir," responded Jerome, slowly.
"Only — I should like to know just what he
is, and just what is best."

Northrop rose hastily. "I must go," he
said. "Come along, my boy. Did you ever
read the story of Hamlet?"

"Often."

"Read it again, read it again. But at any
rate," he continued, when they were safely in
the carriage, "you are sure you want to be a
reporter? Perhaps it is as well. We shall see
what we can do for you. Maybe you can help
against Wheeler sometimes; that ought to

please you. Unless," he added, sardonically, " you don't think it's for the best."

" I am taking you home," he went on. " I want you to meet my wife and Elsie. You will stay with us — for a time at least?"

But Jerome demurred. " I have my own way to make," he explained. " I haven't much money, of course. You are too good to me as it is. And I think I had better begin as I shall have to continue."

Northrop seemed not displeased. " Well, we shall see," he assented. " Meanwhile report to McKinney — he is the city editor — when you get ready for work. I shall inform him who you are. How much time do you want to get settled and see the town?"

" Twelve hours will be enough. I can report to-morrow afternoon, I think."

" As you please, as you please," the older man replied. " Here we are. I shall introduce you and then run off again to the office."

Mrs. Northrop received Jerome cordially. She was a small, eager woman, vivacious, bright-eyed, much younger than her husband in appearance. She was engaged, she declared, in sorting out the winter things, deciding what

to put away for the next year and what to give
to the poor.

"It is very difficult," she asserted, "to decide in matters of that kind — don't you think
so, Mr. Kent? Because so often one gives
away things that are really *good,* you know,
and then one is sorry afterward."

"Why not make a rule to give away only
the worthless articles?" suggested her husband.

"Why, Henry!" she protested. "That
would hardly be charitable — would it, Mr.
Kent?"

"Some time ago," observed Mr. Northrop,
"the method was to keep the best and give
away the rest. But the poor have grown so
discriminating nowadays that one must reverse
the system to keep one's self-respect."

"Why, Henry!" she said again. Northrop
seized his hat — he had not removed his heavy
coat. "Well, I must go," he declared.
"Where's Elsie? Oh, here she is!"

A young girl, rather tall, blue-eyed like her
father, came into the room. She stooped to
kiss him. Jerome saw that she was larger than
either of her parents. When he was presented,

she said nothing, but gave him her hand
quietly. It was cool and firm — like a man's
hand, he thought. Suddenly he became conscious that he was holding it, and dropped it,
blushing. She did not seem to notice his
blush.

"Elsie is very like her father, don't you
think, Mr. Kent?" her mother asked when
Northrop was gone. She stayed not for an
answer, however. "But she is much stronger.
She is very strong; I think she could stand
even a Chicago summer, and you know how
terrible *they* are."

"I do not believe that Mr. Kent is interested in bulletins of my health, mamma," observed Elsie.

"Oh, yes — very much," he declared
quickly, wishing immediately afterward that
he had held his tongue. But Mrs. Northrop,
being now launched, sailed on serenely, heed-
less of small cross-currents.

"We generally go east for the summer —
to Long Branch, or to Europe. I think some
time in Europe is very necessary for a young
girl, don't you? I don't like travelling; but of
course, where one has one's duty — you know

what I mean? One summer we went to Colo-
rado on some fancy of Mr. Northrop's — I
think it was that we should know our own
country. As if one could know it all — or
wanted to! It would be like knowing everybody on the street, don't you think? The unpleasant people as well as the nice ones. I
would rather choose the best and stick to that
— wouldn't you? But Mr. Northrop has odd
ideas. He never goes with us, you know; he
prefers to stay in town and work, and then
spend his Sundays at Lake Forest. We have
a place there, you know; oh, only a little one.
But he is very fond of it. I used to like it
years ago. But Lake Forest is common ground
now; everybody goes there, you know. One
might as well stay in the city, almost — don't
you think so, Mr. Kent?"

Elsie sat quietly, her hands in her lap. Jerome thought he had never seen any one so
calm. She seemed almost to exhale the chill
of marble. He wondered whether she resented
her mother's loquacity, which amused him and
pleased him at the same time, since it relieved
him of the necessity of conversing. As he
looked about the room, the contrast inevitably

presented itself between this and his mother's
one-storied rambling white house on the edge
of the Indiana village — the house that was his
no longer.   Both houses were clambered over
by vines; but there the resemblance closed.
The vines on the Kent cottage were morning-
glories, unregulated, profuse, now shot with
flaring bells of purple, crimson, and white, now
raggedly trailing off in their green streamers.
Here the vines were ivy, carefully tended, thick
and close; ivy that grew all the year round, he
fancied, as Dickens's ivy did.   These were the
vines of elegance.   And the room itself —
large, white-and-gold, emitting an atmosphere
of costliness; Jerome was connoisseur enough
to guess that the spindling chairs in this room
alone were worth more than all their furniture.
This house, with its fineness, its richness, its
comfort; the coachman, the butler who had
awed him at the door, the man who brought the
tea — they might all have been his mother's,
had she willed to marry Northrop. Would she
have willed so had she known? And in that
case where would this little, elegant, bustling
woman who was just then telling him of the
hotel in Florence, on the Lung' Arno, in which

they had passed a winter amidst the glories of
the Renaissance — a hotel which actually had
hot running water, and a lift that would take
you down as well as up — where would this
unconscious little woman be? And the girl
opposite him; and he himself? At this point
in his wonderings he laughed.

"Oh, I assure you there was nothing funny
about it — not in the least," she smiled at him
brightly. "We hadn't the *least* idea where we
were — not the least in the world; and the
courier of course had always done the talking,
so we didn't know a word of Italian. It's very
foolish to learn so many languages, don't you
think so? Because here in America one has
no chance to practise them. Oh, French, of
course everybody should know French, don't
you think so? But as I was saying — " She
went on to tell of her Florentine adventure,
which threatened tragic things, but which
ended when Elsie, her attention being called
to the situation by her distracted mother,
had had the brilliant idea of summoning a carriage and telling the driver the name of their
hotel; to which he promptly conveyed them in
safety. "But I never should have thought of

that in the world," Mrs. Northrop insisted. Meanwhile, again Jerome congratulated himself that his discourteous thoughts had not been noticed, and determined to pay strict attention for the remainder of the afternoon. He could not help wondering, however, whether the daughter had seen his embarrassment. But she gave no sign. He was still wondering when they delivered him into the hands of a servant, who showed him the room in which he was to prepare himself for dinner.

"Only come down whenever you are ready," she added. "I think you will like the library — don't you think Mr. Kent will like the library, Elsie?"

The room into which he was shown interested him so much that time passed without his being aware. That it was a guest-chamber he could scarcely believe, for the walls were hung with engravings and one copy — in oil — of a Puvis de Chavannes; and the books were neither uncut, shabby, nor uninteresting. He picked out at random a thin volume of Maeterlinck, and read it, standing by the window, until the light failed him. Then suddenly he became conscious that it was late, and he

washed himself hurriedly, resuming perforce
the same collar and tie, but wishing he had
brought another in his pocket. He scarcely
liked to venture into the hallway, for he had
no idea where the "library" was placed.
Therefore he sat down to wait until he was
called. He would have turned on the electric
light, but he was unable to discover the button.
So he sat in the twilight until some one knocked
and he followed the footman obediently to
dinner.

He had expected that in such a house the
family would dine in evening dress, he told
himself; still his own comparative unconven-
tionality intruded itself suddenly when he was
seated opposite Elsie. To his mind she and
her mother were gowned as for a grand ball;
and Northrop looked more finely cut, more
delicate, more patrician than ever in his careful
evening clothes. For a moment Jerome, in involuntary resentment, reminded himself that
this man, like himself, was born in a small,
straggling Indiana town; that at his own age,
indeed; this man had probably never seen a city
of thirty thousand people, and certainly had
never heard of the contemporary Maeterlincks,

E

or Puvis de Chavannes! But two minutes of
Northrop's company made him forget all that.

"I have been reading Maeterlinck," he confessed, when they had proceeded some way
into the dinner. "I found a book of his in
my room."

"You poor boy!" cried Mrs. Northrop, sym-
pathetically. "Was that all you had there?
I shall tell Julius to-morrow to see that something good is put in that room."

"No, no," Jerome protested. "There were
other books. But I had heard of him, and I
was very much interested. He is remarkable,
don't you think so? I was reading the 'Hazard
of New Fortunes' in the train last night.
That is remarkable too. It comforts one, it
seems to me, to think sometimes that we needn't
all be remarkable in the same way."

"Did Maeterlinck write the 'Hazard of New
Fortunes'?" cried Mrs. Northrop. "I always
thought Henry James wrote that."

There was a slight pause, very much embarrassed on Jerome's part. Elsie was serene,
Northrop quiet. .

"I believe it was written by Mr. Howells,"
Jerome said finally. "But possibly it was
James."

" Oh, no," cried Mrs. Northrop again, gayly.
" I meant Howells, of course. But I never can
remember which is which, you know."

" At school," added Elsie, suddenly, " Miss
Wayland had an idea that Maeterlinck was a
Frenchman, and so she forbade us to read him.
He was very popular then. But I think he has
gone out now." She relapsed again into silence and Jerome was again puzzled. Was she
serious, or laughing at them all? He planned,
if he had opportunity, to study her, and put
her in his story, provided she was really not so
simple as at first sight she seemed. He lay
awake that night for some time, thinking out
the events of the day, and wondering whether
he should ever get leisure any more to work
upon his novel. In the morning he opened his
eyes upon a new life.

CHAPTER II

JEROME regarded with a half proprietary interest the *Eagle* office. The swinging door let
him into a scene of commerce, of finance, of
anything but the business of a newspaper.
High desks stood all about, fenced by gratings
and frosted glass. At this hour, just after
midday, most of them were untenanted; but a
few clerks still busied themselves with ledgers
or long files. Jerome said to one: —

"I should like to see Mr. McKinney."

"Don't know him," answered the clerk,
with an accent, neither polite nor wholly impolite, which might be called American.

"He is the city editor."

"Sixth floor, then," replied the clerk, looking up. "This is the business office. You
want the editorial rooms."

At the sixth floor the attendant, blonde,
plainly a Swede, but at one with the clerk in
that touch-me-not air so pervasive of our whole

life of trade, from the captain of industry to the least private, jerked out a further direction, "631 — third right." 631 proved to be a kind of main entrance, or hallway — a long room lined with stalls in frosted glass. On the sliding door of each stall was a number and a title in black — 634, City Editor; 635, Copy Readers; 636, Sporting Editor, and so on. Beyond lay another room, larger, apparently empty. The city editor's stall was empty also; so were they all. Presently, however, as he stood uncertainly, two men emerged from the room beyond.

"Yes, pretty good," one continued, a stout slouchy man in shirtsleeves. His voice came indistinctly around an unlit cigar, which he chewed and flirted from side to side as he talked.

"Well, how much?" demanded the other man in a tone of satisfaction.

"Oh, you know as well as I do, Donahue, — a stickful, maybe two sticks."

"I've been out on it all morning," grumbled Donahue, a thin-faced, sandy-haired, unpleasantly sallow Irishman.

"Make it three hundred words then," answered the stout man, impatiently.

" And have you cut the liver out of it, hey ? "

Donahue retired sourly to the back room, whence came presently the intermittent clatter of a typewriter. The fat man retired into the den marked City Editor, without seeming to notice Jerome. Through an open door Jerome could see him savagely cutting and mangling, with a sweeping pair of shears, a pile of newspapers that lay upon the desk. He was really finishing the important part of his day's work, though Jerome did not know it; extracting from the morning issues of all the city papers such matter as seemed to him worth devoting the further attention of some reporter to. After some time, as he still continued without cessation to read and cut, Jerome ventured to interrupt him.

" Is this the city editor ? "

" Yes; what can I do for you ? "

" My name is Kent. I was told by Mr. Northrop to report to you at noon to-day."

" Oh — you're the man." The city editor looked Jerome over, tilting his cigar against the point of his nose. " Ever work on a paper ? I suppose not."

" I'm a printer," Jerome answered cau-

tiously. " But," he added, " I've never worked
on a daily."

" Eau Claire, Keokuk, Sandwich, or Ko-
komo?"

" I beg your pardon?"

" Where are you from?" translated the city
editor.

" Scannell County, Indiana."

" So? I've been there myself. I went to
school at Valparaiso. When the boys here
can't get a fake past me they tell me I was born
in Kansas, raised in Indiana, and live in En-
glewood. They think I'm a Reuben — fatally
Reuben. Do you know Chicago?"

" No, sir."

" Well, go in and sit down. I'll give you
an assignment presently."

With no more formality Kent found himself
a member of the staff of the *Eagle*. Mr. Mc-
Kinney fell once more to clipping newspapers,
and Jerome retired to the back room, where
the sallow Donahue was still hammering the
groaning typewriter.

The door of this apartment bore the single
word " Reporters." The room was square,
and of good size. Around three sides ran a

ledge or bench, some three feet high, littered with coarse paper, and occupied every two yards by a typewriting machine. On the fourth side, on either hand of the door, stood two huge oblong pine tables. Light wooden chairs lay promiscuously about, more paper littered the floor and filled several large waste-baskets, and over each machine a bulbous electric light dangled from a cord, like a fat spider. Three or four notices posted on the walls, and a certain complement of spittoons, completed the furniture of the room. The streaming sun added to the untidiness of the place.

For lack of other entertainment Jerome fell to examining the notices. The largest, in defiant type, prohibited smoking, in smaller letters apologetically laying the blame upon an insurance company. Another, headed " Days off," much mutilated and changed, gave a list of the reporters, with the day of the week assigned to each as vacation. A third, which Jerome, after reading, copied for his own pleasure, contained " Rules."

1. Do not use the awkward expression " as though." Say " as if."

2. Do not spit on the floor. (To this was

added, in pencil, "Reserved for the City
Editor.")

3. The *Eagle* spells it *tho*.

4. December 12, *not* December 12th.

While Jerome was still copying, Donahue
looked up.

"New man?" he remarked.

"I hope so," Jerome replied.

"Humph! Got a chew?"

"Of tobacco?" inquired Jerome. Donahue
favoured him with a long stare and a grin.

"No, gum," he answered finally. "Never
mind. Where'd you work before?"

"Nowhere," answered Jerome, peacefully.
He wondered if Donahue was the final bloom
of that evolutionary process technically known
as "turning reporter." The Irishman's next
words seemed conclusive.

"I've worked on every paper in town," he
boasted. "When I get tired here, I slide over
to the *Star*. They all know me. I can get a
job anywhere." He picked up his manuscript
and rose. "You look like you'd make a good
reporter; look as if you had nerve. That's all
it takes — just nerve. You go up to a man
and beg of him and he'll throw you down every

time; laugh at you. But you go in and say,
'Look here, old boy, here's something I've got
to have, see?' Just bluff right up to him, see?
and you'll get him all right, all right. That's a
tip. Oh, you'll do all right. All you want is
somebody to put you on." The reporter threw
out his thin chest. Plainly, he considered
himself " on." On what? Life as a reporter
began to seem less agreeable. Donahue
started out; then, struck by a sudden idea, returned.

" Say," he remarked confidentially, " to-
morrow's pay-day, and of course I'm broke this
afternoon. Lend me a quarter, will you? "

" Wouldn't a dollar do as well? " questioned
Jerome.

" Why, sure! "

" Or five cents? " pursued Jerome placidly.

Donahue threw him an ugly look. " Oh,
hell! " he replied, leaving the room.

Presently other reporters began coming in.
One or two glanced at him, but most seemed to
ignore him. The chief impression he gained
from watching them was that they were an
untidy lot. Presently a demoniac shriek
whistled through the room. Jerome started,

but a man stepped very calmly to one of the
pine tables, and picked up a tube that lay upon
it. " Well? "

" Harmon," came a sepulchral voice.

" Harmon, you're wanted," said the reporter
at the tube, turning away. One of the older
men passed out.

Of those who remained, some read newspapers — usually the *Eagle,* Jerome observed
— now and then cutting out a fragment and
stuffing the remainder in a waste-basket.
Others pecked at the keys of the writing ma-
chines. The rest talked in low voices. Everything they discussed fell under two heads —
newspaper " shop," *i.e.* business; or news
of some kind of sport. Nobody in the room
looked over thirty, few over twenty-five. Jerome felt an access of years as he watched
them. He wondered if all reporters were very
young men, concluding (erroneously) that as
they aged they must be appointed to editorial
positions. Meanwhile the tubes shrieked inter-
mittently, and the group of a dozen or four-
teen rapidly lessened. After some time Jerome
found himself alone. He looked at his watch;
it was a quarter to two. He wondered if he was

forgotten. The wild scream cut into the silence of the room once more, and he advanced, laughing at his own trepidation, to pick the tube up. " Well ? "   " Kent," said a voice, before he could put the tube to his ear. He dropped it and hurried out to the city editor's stall. The city editor, as before, was chewing an unlit cigar. From its damp and battered appearance, Jerome judged it the same cigar.

" Now," the fat man declared, without looking up, " I've got just the assignment for you." His voice was soothing and cordial. " I want you to go up to the John Kocynski School and find out about an entertainment they're going to give to-morrow night. Look it up carefully ; don't forget the details, or you'll have to go back. Imagine yourself one of those Polacks up there, and find out what you'd want to know in that case. We've got a big circulation in that district, and they like to see themselves noticed. You said you didn't know your way about the town ? "

" I can find it."

" Here."   McKinney showed him a large map on the wall. " The school is at the corner of Lena and McArthur, out Humboldt Park way." He traced a possible course with a stubby forefinger, the nail in deep mourning. " Take the Elston Avenue car and get off at McArthur. I'll give you car tickets." He tore off a few from a strip like a bicycle chain. " Better take four. Now get along, and be back as soon as you can." McKinney's manner was paternal.

Jerome went out on his first assignment, in ignorance how to get the news, but determined not to return until he had it. After some inquiry he found the Elston Avenue car, and inquired for McArthur Street. Yes, they passed it. How soon? In about half an hour, said the conductor, jerking the bell. They bumped and clattered slowly through the business district. Once over the river, they proceeded faster and more smoothly. They sped past blocks and blocks where, among the innumerable signs, never a name of Anglo-Saxon origin rewarded the seeker's eye. Crossing the North Branch, they trailed rapidly among yards of coal and lumber; thence emerged again into another region of small shops, whose cheap goods overflowed everywhere out upon the sidewalks; then clanged and spurted through a stretch of tawdry flats, most of them with high basements and unsteady stairways crawling up to the front door. Leaving these in turn behind, they darted boldly out into wide spaces, where forlorn signs stood alone — "For Sale. Apply to John Blank." They stopped infrequently. At last the conductor turned to Jerome, who had for some time been straining his eyes in the attempt to discern somewhere McArthur Street.

"McArthur next."

The car slowed; Jerome swung off; in a moment the rocking electric chariot was spinning twenty miles an hour along the rails. Jerome felt unreasonably lonely as he watched it depart.

Lena Street he knew lay to the west. He strode off along the sidewalk, which here ran on stilts eight feet above the ground. Primeval prairie seemed to lie about him — a vast acreage of weeds. Yet in five minutes' walk he found himself among numerous houses. Another square, and he came upon a big, oblong, red-brick, tomblike structure, picked out with white. A gravelled yard surrounded as much of it as he could see. A glance at the lamp-post confirmed his suspicion that he had reached Lena Street and the John Kocynski School.

He entered the bare, empty hall, and after a few minutes' hesitation knocked at one of the doors. It opened. A glimpse of fifty small faces — fifty pairs of eyes levelled at his — then he confronted the teacher. She was Jewish and quite pretty.

"You should see the principal," she answered, when Jerome had put the case to her. "He will be glad to tell you. I will take you there." She looked at Jerome sidewise, and led the way upstairs, dilatory, questioning him on each step. He was a relief in the slow day. Besides, he had looked at her with approval. She left him at the second floor, after pointing out the right office.

"Just wait till I go down, will you?" she asked. "He doesn't like us to leave our rooms." She tripped down, looking back at him over her shoulder. He remembered her face — dark, coquettish, with a little scar over one eye, like a heart.

The principal gladly furnished all the details Jerome asked for. He said it was very kind of the *Eagle* to inquire. He himself read the *Eagle* always; yes, always. He was dark-haired, a foreigner of some kind, probably a Pole. Just a trace of some native accent remained in his voice. There was one slight mistake, he said; the entertainment was yesterday evening, not to-morrow. " Be sure," he said, " to put that right — yesterday." He himself had made a little talk, had said thus and so. Jerome soon felt himself master of every detail in connection with the event.

The pretty Jewess awaited him in the lower hall. " Did you get what you wanted?" she inquired pleasantly.

" Yes, thank you."

" It's a long way up here, isn't it? "

" Yes, it is rather far."

" I live much nearer town — on West Adams, 7777 is the number — four sevens."

" Miss Goldberg! " The principal's voice, menacing, came over the banisters. Miss Goldberg jumped and retreated to her room, not without a backward look. Jerome went away smiling. While he waited for the car that should return him to the office, he saw afar off the Kocynski School disgorging its pupils. He looked at his watch; it was half-past three.

The city editor, refreshed by a clean cigar, greeted him pleasantly.

" Well, what'd you find? "

Jerome described the entertainment graphically.

" Two sticks," interrupted McKinney.

" By the way," said Jerome, turning, " the entertainment was last night, not to-morrow."

" Why didn't you say so? " answered the city editor. " Never mind, then."

" What shall I do? "

" Nothing. Well — write out an announcement — twenty words."

Those twenty words took Jerome as many minutes. When he brought them in he laid down also two car tickets. " I didn't use these," he remarked.

McKinney struggled with himself. His wide blue eyes seemed brimming over with a stare. " That's right," he said finally, " always return what you don't use. By the way," he added, " this is script. You must learn the typewriter. Go in and practise now, till dinner time. Come back after dinner."

F

Jerome practised, went out to dine — on two sandwiches and a cup of coffee; ten cents — and returned. There was, however, no assignment for him that evening, and at half-past nine the night city editor told him he might as well go home. Next morning he eagerly searched for the " story " of the afternoon before. He found it at last — the first item under the column " City Happenings." Here is his day's work in print: —

" The pupils of the John Kocynski School, Lena and McArthur streets, gave their annual concert on Tuesday evening."

Now Jerome received sometimes one assignment a day, sometimes two. They led him into all quarters of the city. He learned where Maxwell Street is; that Emerald Avenue is not named for the greenness of its grass and trees; that not all Chicago boulevards are asphalted. One day he passed, by pure chance, 7777 West Adams Street, and laughed over the naïveté which conducts social forms among some of us. One day he was sent to see a doctor, who wished to air a grievance against the County Hospital; but it turned out to be a matter of dollars and cents, and the *Eagle*

would not print it. One day he " followed up "
the " City Press " account of a small fight in an
outlying saloon, McKinney fancying the sur-
roundings might give opportunity for a " descriptive story " — might be effectively treated
as a bit of local life. The saloon, lonely, a
wooden building, surrounded by wide vacant
lots, interested Jerome, but McKinney said,
when he heard what it was like, " Thousands
of 'em. No good." One day he went into the
suburbs, on a " tip " that a farmer near Wash-
ington Heights had discovered oil in his barn-
yard. The rumour was true; but unfortunately
for Jerome it was spread abroad in the early
morning, so that the afternoon papers of the
same day, discussing the event fully, killed his
story. On Sunday Jerome collected and pasted
end to end all the items he had printed. The
brevity of the string dashed him. His pay,
they said, would be six dollars a column. He
had calculated, when he learned the rate, that
should he by his own efforts fill even so little
as a column a day, he would nevertheless receive a weekly salary of thirty-six dollars. But
when the cashier handed him his check it was
for three dollars and forty cents. He hoped for
better luck as time went on.

He cashed the check at the Union National.
A carriage was drawn up by the curb before
the bank, and as Jerome passed a man descended the steps — a man who made Jerome's
six feet look small. His face was coarse and
powerful. He might have been a hippopotamus in a frock coat. His voice rumbled when
he spoke to his coachman.

"Yessir, yessir."

Growling, the hippopotamus stumped into
the bank. The coat opening disclosed a wide
and richly ornamented waistcoat, crossed by
heavy golden links, which supported ornaments
massive and barbaric. Crushing through the
door, he demanded "Mr. Cahill." "In his
office waiting for you, sir." The big man
shouldered around the corner of the railing.

"Do you know that man?" asked Jerome,
laying his check before a teller.

"Endorse it — here." The teller slid it
back.

"The big man with the frock coat and the
red hair," repeated Jerome.

"Three-forty." The teller pushed out three
silver dollars and some small change. "Don't
block the window, please," he said curtly.
"That's the vice-president."

" What is his name? "

The teller stared. " Christopher Wheeler," he admitted, after a pause.

Jerome moved on. He looked at the three silver dollars in his hand. That oppressive bulk, the gold of that watch-chain, this brisk employee who asked Jerome not to block the window, were Wheeler's. Well, here was a dollar to offset each. Jerome laughed.

CHAPTER III

WHEELER went on into the private office of
the president. Cahill, a short, spare man with
bushy whiskers over a masklike face, rose to
greet him.

" Something special? "

" Yes." Wheeler sat down heavily. " The
meeting is to-morrow, hey? Well, I'm going
to pull out."

Cahill's face betrayed no emotion. " Do
you intend to leave the directorate? "

" Yes, I'm going to pull out."

" Sudden, isn't it? " remarked the president,
after a pause.

" Oh, I reckon you knew it was coming —
hey? "

" I? why should I? "

" It's mostly you that I'm leaving for," replied Wheeler, savagely. " I don't mind telling
you, I don't altogether like the way things are
run here."

70

Cahill busied himself with a paper, and his sharp eyes showed no gleam. The two men were notoriously at variance in their ideals. He had expected a break before. But the situation was unexpectedly simple; Wheeler retired without a fight! Cahill at the moment experienced the emotion of a general who has for months advanced his siege-lines, only, on the critical day, to find the city wholly deserted, the frowning batteries wooden. But satisfaction dominated. He had been sure of winning, yet certainly Wheeler was a redoubtable antagonist.

"Send somebody for my box, will you?" demanded Wheeler. When it was brought he unlocked it and began looking over various certificates. Cahill returned to his desk. He wondered why Wheeler was backing down. Presently the clerk of the outer office opened the door tentatively, and Cahill looked up.

"Miss Robertson is waiting, Mr. Cahill, shall I tell her you are busy? She says she has an appointment."

Cahill glanced at Wheeler.

"Send her in," growled the big man. Cahill nodded to the clerk. In a moment Miss Robertson appeared. Cahill rose, but Wheeler remained doggedly busy with his papers.

"How do you do, Mr. Cahill?" she greeted him. "You got my note?"

"Yesterday. Will you sit down?"

"Of course you know then that I am on business, and I needn't keep you long. Can you help us?"

"Isn't your original scheme branching out a good deal?" Cahill asked.

"I hope so," she smiled. "You don't condemn live things for growing, Mr. Cahill?"

"Well — no. But I should like a few more particulars — if you have time."

"Have you?"

"Yes. But perhaps we had better take the other office." He did not look at Wheeler. But the vice-president from among his papers, grumbled "No." Miss Robertson did not seem to notice him; she began to speak, however, at once. She laid her plans out in some detail. They were connected with a day-nursery for a "College Settlement," far up in the northwest quarter of the town.

"In short," she went on, "to interest the mothers it is absolutely necessary to capture the young children. I suppose one looking only to the future could have hope, even if the mothers were abandoned to their fate. But it seems to me that many of our plans concern themselves too much with speculation for the future, and not enough with amelioration of the present. Besides, the mothers interest me. And so," she concluded, " the nursery seems an absolute present necessity."

" I never argue with you when I can help it, Miss Robertson," acquiesced Cahill, " for I find I am always beaten, and I dislike being beaten."

" But like a true sportsman, you own up," she laughed.

" You shall not flatter me into another penny," he declared. " You asked for five hundred?" She rose as he handed her the check.

" I'll give you a thousand," said Wheeler. Even the careful face of Cahill showed his surprise. Wheeler rose. " A thousand," he repeated.

" Mr. Christopher Wheeler, Miss Robertson," said the president, recovering. The lady bowed; Wheeler gave a slight nod.

" Give me a check, Cahill," he remarked.

But Miss Robertson had recovered from her astonishment.

" Will you come and see me first, Mr. Wheeler? " she asked calmly.

" Hey? "

" Please come and see me before you send me the check. Or — I will call at your office some other time."

Wheeler's pen paused. " Why not now? "

Miss Robertson was silent. Wheeler filled out the check.

" Here," he said. But she made no movement to accept it. Suddenly the rare glow came into Cahill's eyes. He had stood watching, unsmiling, a spectator at a play he did not understand. Now he understood and was bitterly amused.

" Before me, too — the last man Chris would want there," he thought. But he gave no sign.

" I can't take it, Mr. Wheeler," the lady said finally. He could not understand. " Isn't my money as good as anybody else's? " he demanded. She was silent. A slow perception crept into the great man's brain.

"Well, by —— !" he said, under his breath; then broke off, stared at the check, tore it twice, flung the pieces into the grate, and moved back to his chair.

"I am very sorry to seem melodramatic, Mr. Wheeler, but indeed you brought it on yourself," Miss Robertson said, with spirit. "But believe me, I am very sorry." Her voice softened. The big man slouching together in his big chair had nevertheless to her something of the air of the ill-used schoolboy. "Won't you come and talk it over with me — at my house?" she added. Wheeler grunted, but was unintelligible. In a moment Miss Robertson took her leave, and Cahill, at her request, followed her out.

"I suppose I need not ask you not to tell any one about this," she remarked.

"It will do him good to have it known."

"I confess," she returned with a smile, "I was thinking of myself. I am afraid it is too theatrical. So please, Mr. Cahill." The president reluctantly promised.

When he returned Wheeler was on his feet. The papers were in their box. "Send that back, will you?" he growled. "I shall sell out to-morrow." He made no mention of the incident that had passed.

Cahill, a moment later, stepped into another room.

" Will! "

" Well, father? "

" Wheeler has just been in."

" I thought," observed the young man at the desk, " that I heard the old bear growling."

" He is going to sell his stock and retire," went on the president, casually.

" The deuce he is! "

" So he says, Will. He objects to our methods." The eyes of the two men met, and the younger laughed. But Cahill showed his usual lack of expression.

" He has the virtues and the faults of all men with tremendous conceit," the son remarked. " They carry everything before them for a while, then they think 'the world is mine,' and down they go like the middle pin. Look at Napoleon, for instance, or Bismarck. I don't mean to be personal, father."

" I suppose you'll take the vice-presidency," replied Cahill, irrelevantly. He would have

liked to tell his son the story of the afternoon.

Wheeler, too, was thinking of it as he drove
about. At the office of the gas company he
ordered the superintendent to fill a vacant place
among the stenographers with a girl whose
name and address he gave. This attention to
detail occasioned no surprise; it was Wheeler's
custom to interfere in little matters, discharging
one man for coming five minutes late, promot-
ing another who held the door open as he
passed.

" There was a woman in here to see you to-
day," said the superintendent. " She waited
awhile, then she began to make a fuss, and we
had to put her out. She left her name for you;
here it is. I thought I'd tell you."

The big man looked at the name — " Etta
Goldberg, 7777 West Adams." " *She* came
round, did she? Don't know her," he said
aloud. " I'll stop her coming round again," he
thought, profanely.

It was the incident in Cahill's office that
carried him to his lawyers', where he demanded to examine his will. It was a document which he was constantly changing and

shifting in little things. Now he looked it over with care.

"Wouldn't take my money!" he thought. He had no resentment, only a marvellous wonderment at her foolishness. He was still so entirely incapable of Miss Robertson's point of view that a sort of dull sadness grew up in him, which even the provisions of his will lost their power to dissipate. Suppose the trustees of the institution which — and what an utter astonishment it was to be to everybody! — he intended to enrich with memorials at his death —suppose they refused his money, as this little woman had refused it to-day? Was he to be balked in the end of the satisfaction he anticipated; prevented of his ambitions, because people hated a successful man? He had taken the world by the throat, and the world disliked him accordingly. Some such thought mistily formed in his big brain.

He drove on his way back to the office to see the doctor. A hoarseness in his breathing had annoyed him for some time, and though he disliked doctors he determined to have it removed. But the physician shook his head at the peremptory demand.

"My dear sir," he said, "we can't do things in just that way. I wish we could. But you are the only man who can do anything for yourself. You have lived a great deal in your time, you see; now the machinery would naturally run a little more slowly, and yet you force it ahead constantly. Slacken it." He would not prophesy an end, "except general collapse, if you don't take care of yourself." Wheeler grunted again.

He was so far from understanding that which had happened to him at the bank, that he narrated the incident at dinner. In telling it, his wonderment appeared in a kind of grim gusto — that there should be such idiots. His wife, a trodden, striving creature, who had almost managed the difficult feat of forgetting their past, felt less amusement and more anger.

"Of course the woman wants more out of you!" she cried. "Didn't she tell you to come and see her? You mark my word, Christopher, she will be at you again before long." Only his daughter felt any shame, and she concealed it, as she was accustomed to conceal her feeling in this one regard. The youngest of the group, she was the only one to whom their anomalous position in the world, the constant abuse of the newspapers, and such infrequent happenings as this, raised any doubts of the family ethics. She had spent four years in a boarding school in the East, in a sylvan spot of Massachusetts to which all Chicago was only a bustling and unpleasant noise in the distance; where her father's fame and his notoriety were equally unknown. There she had been accepted for herself, a girl among girls. At first she attracted some attention by the excessive smartness of her clothes, but she was infinitely adaptable in small things, and soon she merged into the habits of the rest, and was one of them. Her vacations she had spent in the East, or travelling abroad after the fashion of Americans. Thus she had never known, or guessed, that her father's methods were criticised in his home. She knew or vaguely remembered that he was not like the fathers of some of the other girls whom she had met, but he was idealized as time went on, and distance continued its process of enchantment. He had been besides a good father to her. Indeed, in his own household he growled least of anywhere. His wife tacitly allowed him certain liberties; in return he recognized the rights of his family to some extent. He was used, it was true, to fly into ungovernable rages. During one of these, some time before, he had gone so far as to strike his wife with his fist. But the sobering remembrance remained with him, and even in his utmost fury, now, he used no physical violence toward human beings — even the servants. But it was woe to the pet dog who crossed his path in some hours, or the chair that stood unluckily at his hand. These moments of passion were becoming more and more frequent as he grew older and more overbearing in his success. It was one of them, occurring shortly after her arrival from boarding school, that first set his daughter to sorrowful wonder. What was the matter with her father? Was it possible that this unrestrained half-maniac who drove the white-faced footman from the room, and sent her mother flying in terror to lock herself in her own apartments — was the man of whom, latterly, she had boasted to her friends? As she lived on, too, she quickly began to notice the rigid limits of their social place. Her mother complained querulously or bitterly of the "stuck up" family

G

of Haywards, whom she despised. The cause
of her contempt, it soon appeared, was simple;
they ignored her. It was a new thought to
Miss Wheeler that she might be ignored by
any one in Chicago whom she chose to know.
The Haywards were only typical; they multi-
plied themselves into a list, and on that list
she found the names of one or two or three
whose daughters she had known at Pitthamp-
ton, over whose adoration for her no shadow
of doubt had fallen. Now they asked her to
their homes, but they did not come to hers.
Thus she gradually found herself forced into a
kind of loneliness, not disagreeable to her in
itself, but unpleasant in its mysterious cause.
There were families in Chicago, then, that
shunned the Wheelers. Why? Her mother's
creed was easy; they were envious, resentful,
"stuck up." But the explanation did not
wholly satisfy Miss Wheeler. She declined,
in spite of her mother's insistence, to "come
out" at once; she must wait a little, she said,
until she was grown up. Her mother, futilely
impatient, yielded without knowing why.

This refusal of Miss Robertson's, then,
struck the young girl with a proud shame. She

was indignant for a moment; but soon the indignation gave place to a suffusal of sorrow. Miss Robertson! They said she had no enemies even among the men whose work she tried to undo; they said she was the best citizen of the city. And this woman had refused her father's money, the girl thought, as if it were polluted! Ethel Wheeler, in her six months in Chicago, had learned more, perhaps, than in all her years of boarding school. This lesson now came to complete her education. Yet it is doubtful if she needed it. She had passed already the stage in which she wondered " why." Now her query was, " But what am I to do? " She went up to her own room and cried.

CHAPTER IV

JEROME had taken lodgings, as Northrop
suggested, on the North side — on Huron
Street, in a large, ugly brick house so filled
with lodgers like himself that the family of the
landlord was crowded into the basement. The
landlord himself, a certain Mr. Kenealy, Jerome
had never seen; all business had been trans-
acted with the landlord's wife, a tall martinet
with a darting eye that put one immediately in
the wrong. Mrs. Kenealy, in twenty years'
experience of letting rooms, had dealt with
men and women of all kinds, and like the rest
of us in a similar case, she paid tribute of suspicion to all humanity. She was taciturn; she
possessed the silence of the Indian, whose custom is to lie in wait. Mrs. Kenealy was not
to be deceived by easy manners, nor appeased
by tales of misfortune; one paid (in advance)
or left the house. But, as she exacted rigidly,
so she gave exactly what she said. To this

woman three clean towels a week meant three clean towels. Oh, upright Mrs. Kenealy! it would be pleasant to stay a moment to sing her praises — the praise of a landlady whose towels were double length. But a girl is waiting by the lake.

Jerome christened his room the sardine box. It contained the usual furniture in so small a compass that he must fold up his bed if he wished to sit at his table. Here he rose every morning between nine and half-past. He breakfasted on coffee and toast for five cents, in a tiny restaurant on Chicago Avenue, kept by a tiny old lady who sat all day knitting in the window, as dainty as the petals of her own rose-geraniums beside her. He bought the *Eagle* 'regularly; it was his one extravagance, he said. The fact is, he could not wait until he reached the office, at one o'clock, to find out what words of his the hundred thousand subscribers were reading that day. He always read it over the coffee, sometimes cutting out some work of his own, and sometimes finding nothing that he recognized. Afterward, he regularly walked to the lake, and up by Lincoln Park, where the sea-wall stretches to the north, backed by its broad stone promenade. The lake always attracted him, whether it was lying like a monstrous unflawed turquoise, in perfect and wonderful stillness, or whether it fretted and mumbled like an impatient child, at the embankment's foot, or whether it flung itself in masses of solid water and spray against the wall. Sometimes it spread in one colour — pale blue or gray; sometimes it lay stretched like agate, here green, there almost pink, there almost purple. If he came early, he saw the big excursion steamers hurtling to Milwaukee before a trailing smoke that in the alchemy of nature was changed to filmy Point de Venise, and added just the embroidered touch that the sky pattern seemed to need. Or if these had passed, dots of black might crawl far out, like flies on a gigantic window pane — lumber schooners from Menominee, or wheat ships for Buffalo. He would stride briskly up and down, breathing long breaths, clearing his lungs for the day's work, and staring eagerly at the quiet panorama. The sea-wall was his gymnasium and his picture gallery.

On these mornings of May and early June there were few people by the lake. Ubiquitous

baby carriages loitered up and down, or a bicy-
clist rested a few moments from his strained
pedalling, to linger on a bench and let the
breeze cool him. These comers varied from
day to day. But besides them, Jerome noticed
two or three who seemed habitués of the place.
One, a girl, attracted him particularly. She
came regularly, accompanied only by a small
black-and-tan dog, very ill behaved. When
the walk was even more deserted than usual,
she sometimes ran after this dog — not so fast
as he, but with incomparably more grace of
motion. One morning Jerome turned at the
sound of yelping, to find that the chase had
led them almost upon him. She had been unconscious of his presence, but when she saw
him turn, she stopped. At that moment the
mass of her hair, shaken by the run, began to
tumble, and as she put up her hands to it she
caught Jerome's eye. She was young —
younger than her tallness had led him to think.
Instinctively he smiled at her embarrassment;
and she smiled also, and then bit her lip and
looked at the lake. Jerome passed on; he
heard her call the dog, and knew that they had
turned. When he presently faced about again

she was running in the distance. After that he saw her every day. But he could not determine whether she saw him or not.

If Jerome had been a man about town, he might have misinterpreted her smile, and so made a very fatal error. But in the country it is not the custom to be impolite to ladies. Jerome was quite contented to have her in the landscape. Formerly he had come to see the lake, now he came to see the lake, plus this bit of *genre*. So far as he was concerned, the episode might have ended so. He studied her, to reproduce her in his heroine, but his heroine's character he preferred to imagine for himself. Providence, however, and the terrier, decided otherwise.

The park workmen had been mending a part of the wall that the waves had crumbled; they left their work unfinished, however, so that for some time the walk ran unguarded, two feet above the lake. This particular spot the black-and-tan chose, one day, for an attack on Jerome. He circled about, barking furiously, and in his animosity forgot the peril of the edge. Yelping menaces, he backed toward it, and in a moment was over. When the girl came running up, Jerome, flat upon his stomach, was making a long arm to the water. He seized the dripping beast and raised him, shiny but unsubdued, from the lake. The first act of the rescued terrier was to shake himself violently, flirting a halo of drops upon his mistress's gown; the second to bark furiously at his saviour.

"Oh, thank you!" she cried. "Speck, you ungrateful beast, do be still."

"He thinks I pushed him in," explained Jerome.

"It would serve him right if you had," she returned, "you wicked little dog!"

A pause ensued. Jerome was embarrassed, as he was always in the company of women. His life in Indiana had given him no opportunities to study them. To him they were like Byron's love, a thing apart; no more customary and common than strawberries in winter. He had spent much time in wonderment and speculation, for he recognized the difficulty which confronted him, if his heroine were to be flesh-and-blood. But he was no realist; he was not altogether sure he wanted her flesh-and-blood.

Perhaps she pitied his embarrassment; per-

haps she liked his straight body and his fine
eyes; who knows what it was that attracted all
women in Jerome Kent? At all events she
spoke again, and her remark was decisive,
opening the way to acquaintance.

"You come here every day, don't you?"
she asked.

"Yes; I love the lake," he answered. As
he would never have intruded on her acquaintance, so he saw no reason why she should not
form his if she chose. A woman was a fanci-
ful creature whose whims no one could foresee.
"I have seen you often, too," he added.

"I have to give Speck his walk, and this is
the most pleasant walk I know near here."

"I think it is the most pleasant in the whole
world," replied Jerome. He suddenly experienced a curious and welcome exaltation of
spirits, which made his remark seem absolutely
necessary. He looked about; the place was
superlatively fair, he thought. "I used to
know a walk," he went on, "between elms;
they arched the sky out in the middle, but the
sun came in among the trunks, till it was like
ribbons on the road. On one side there were
all the violets in the world, and on the other

just green grass. I used to wonder which side I liked best, and I thought there were no prettier walks than that. But I like this better now."

"Oh!" she cried, "I should like to have seen those violets!"

The black-and-tan punctuated the sentence with furious and explosive barking. He proclaimed his anger to the world. To see those two together confounded him.

"I must go," she said, as though answering the conventional reproof of the black-and-tan. She turned; to his astonishment, Jerome found himself in step beside her. She looked up, and the shyness and the pleasure were written so plainly on his face that she laughed out.

"You are afraid of me," she asserted. "I don't wonder; this is a terrible thing I have done."

For no reason that he could understand, Jerome began to turn red. When she saw it she began to turn red also. There was a horrible pause, then she laughed again, as though she could not stop.

"Oh," she said, "it is too funny! Actually I feel — " but she stopped midway. It was not

till some time afterward that Jerome learned
what she intended to say — "like a kidnap-
per."

"I know perfectly well," she went on finally,
"that I am very foolish. Don't, don't think
that I — that I speak — " She broke off and
looked at him imploringly. "But you were so
funny!"

They were at the south end of the walk now.

"Good-by," she said.

"May I — may I — " stammered Jerome.

"Oh, no, no," she replied, blushing, understanding. "Don't make me hunt another
place to take Speck, please! You see," she
went on, soberly now, "you were so nice that
day when — when my hair came down, and
then you were so fond of the lake, and — I
knew you weren't horrid, you see, so I just — "
she broke off once more. "Can't you just come
as you did, and not notice me? Because I *do*
love the lake, and I *don't* want not to come
here."

"I have noticed you every day," said poor
Jerome.

"Not show it then," she answered quickly.
"I didn't know whether you had or not, you

see. Won't you please?" she begged inconse-
quentially.

"Certainly," replied Jerome. Yes, he
thought, this certainly was a woman; and his
speculations had not been so far from the truth
then!

She walked away, the sunlight turning her
hair to fire as he watched her. She was half
ashamed and half delighted; for she trusted
her guess that this young man was " nice." He
was from the country, she could see at a glance;
and yet he talked, when he was not stammer-
ing, in a fashion she much preferred to the ordinary man's talk that she knew. But certainly
she had run a fearful risk! The light went out
of her face when she thought of it.

He hoped she would turn once before she
walked out of his life as she had walked into it.
But she did not, and he was left to puzzle over
their interview. He puzzled, but it uplifted
him. All day he felt competent to anything —
as though some one he loved had praised him.
That afternoon, as luck had it, brought him his
first assignment of any importance — to cover
a sudden big fire that sprang up in the business
district. For the first time McKinney gave

him a star, and issued curt orders, abandoning the air of paternal solicitude he had hitherto preserved. Even his jocosity dropped away, revealing the best city editor in Chicago. Jerome set out with three other men, so hurriedly he had scarcely time to wonder how to go about the work. But indeed by now his early ignorance of methods was considerably overcome. He was used to the machinery which collects and exhibits news. He knew what " news " was, and could tell beforehand pretty closely how much space McKinney would allow him. He could decide off-hand, too, what was the " feature " of a story — the bit to emphasize. Best of all he was rapidly learning how to observe. In the words of Donahue, the Irishman, he was getting " on."

When Jerome returned with a few facts on his scratch paper and many in his head, McKinney nodded agreeably.

" Now," he said seriously, " Kent, it's up to you. I want you to try your hand at a real good descriptive story. It's just this way: Lawton's down in Danville covering the Wells murder, and Chambers is at the Automobile show, and has got all he can handle. There isn't another first-class descriptive man in the office — unless it's you. I've seen two or three bits in your stuff that make me think you could write if you tried. Now try. Take these facts of yours, and spread yourself. Say first what burnt and who owned it, and then go on to tell what happened — all about it. Make it good, bright, snappy stuff. You've got all the time in the world. For once in my life a man has had the sense to burn up his store at the right hour for us.

"Get in some life now," the city editor went on. "Don't think you're writing a sermon; you aren't."

"It seems to me the simpler the style the better; the facts are enough to carry themselves," remarked Jerome.

"Ah, you're not writing a book now, you're writing for a newspaper," answered McKinney. "You can't say it just the way you want; you've got to say it the way the public wants. Can you do it?"

"Yes."

"Go ahead then."

"How much?"

"Take your own space up to a column and a half. Your story will lead."

Could he do it? There was no doubt in his mind that he could do it. He might stammer now and then with his tongue, but he did not stammer with his pen. His half finished book, on which he spent long hours every Thursday — his day off — represented the chief of Jerome's ambition. He poured himself into that. This newspaper's column-and-half was a bagatelle. He attacked the task eagerly. He recognized the chance he had been unconsciously waiting for. To-day the clamorous typewriter was too slow for his still unskilful fingers, and he scratched away at his pad, tossing sheet after sheet upon a pile. Other men, doing bits of the fire story, or working on other assignments, smacked the keys about him, and came and went, unheeded. McKinney picked up the first sheets, looked them over, and laid them down, satisfied. By seven o'clock the work was done. Jerome stretched himself, handed it in, and went out to dinner, where, as a celebration for the afternoon's chance, he indulged in a steak, of the kind known to the restaurant keepers as a " small."

The next day he woke earlier than usual. He knew that the *Eagle* lay outside his door, as it did every morning, but he preferred to leave it there while he dressed slowly. He pleased himself with foolish fancies — that at the last moment McKinney had decided the story would not do; that some other event of paramount importance had crowded down his work; that the " office " had slashed him out of all recognition. He enjoyed the alternation of feeling, as for a moment he was able to persuade himself of the possibility of these things, and then would realize their unlikelihood.

Frequently, also, the girl by the lake intruded herself upon his mind. He had no intention of speaking to her, of noticing her; he was a man who kept his promises. But still, he rejected two speckless collars, that morning, because their edges were serrated — an imperfection which seldom troubled him much. Moreover, he cast a critical eye over his clothes, and determined, in case he should make any money out of the *Eagle,* to buy himself a new suit as soon as possible. He had been long enough in the city now to know that he had a country air. His trousers, he saw, were undeniably too loose, and seemed to have cheapened in the night. He thought of McKinney's

H

slang on their first meeting, and wondered if he too were " Reuben — fatally Reuben."

When he picked up the *Eagle,* he could not help seeing the headline — " Big Downtown Blaze." Obviously they had given the fire a first page lead. But had they " slashed his story " ? Pleasant tremors coursed up and down his spine, but he would not look yet. He turned into his tiny restaurant, where the tiny old lady sat knitting as usual, as if the eventful yesterday had made no difference to her. She was not even perceptibly older, though it seemed a long time to Jerome since he had breakfasted there the day before. He ordered his coffee and toast deliberately, as usual, of the old lady's granddaughter, who solemnly asked him each morning what he would have, though he had never changed his order. And then he unfolded the *Eagle.*

There was his story. He recognized the opening lines at least. The queer thrill shivered through him, of seeing one's words in clean print; the thrill that is like nothing else in the world; the thrill that makes books without end, as the Song of Solomon says, the thrill that veterans will tell you never quite dies out. He followed the lines down the column. Almost word for word — they had printed his account almost word for word. The office had not slashed him. To be sure they had cut out the semicolons and had changed " although " to " while " in almost every case, but those were trifles. There was his story. " Out of the basement of the four-story building of John King & Company, wholesale dry goods, corner of Clark and Franklin streets, yesterday afternoon at two o'clock, sprang a tongue of flame " — he perused the opening sentence once more. McKinney had insisted that the information should go into the first words, and Jerome had yielded. But the rest he thought was better.

He let the coffee and the toast chill while he read on — twice through the whole account. But he ate them without distaste—his thoughts were far away. He knew enough of the paper to be sure his future was in his own hands now. He could be, in time and with Northrop's backing, what he pleased among the reporters. This single story would give him stamp. But was his ambition to be a reporter? He knew that it was not. To write, to write — but be-

tween covers! Some day it would come. Then
his mind strayed back to the present. He
jumped up hastily. Certainly he would not
speak to her, would not notice her — but it
would be pleasant, nevertheless, to see her
again! There is a fashion decried as inelegant
by the elegant metropolitan arbiters of style,
which prevails in certain sections of the United
States; it is this: a wife speaks of her husband, or a husband of his wife, by the single
personal pronoun only — as " he," or " she."
This unconscious method of indication that to
them one personality blots out all the rest, Jerome involuntarily employed. Would she, he
wondered, be there as usual? He quickened
his steps. If she were not! — But when he
reached the sea-wall, there she was, passing se-
dately, with the terrier trotting quietly behind.
He must inevitably encounter her, then. Could
he maintain the appearance of unconsciousness
which he had promised? The whole situation
struck him, somehow, as foolish and absurd.
Why should he not speak to this young woman,
who liked him, whom he liked? Why should
he not tell her, if she would be interested, in
his triumph of the day before; find out from

her what he must know about some woman, if his heroine were to live?   There were a thousand good reasons for speaking to her, for knowing her, and only one against. He had promised. Well, life is a queer sort.

He approached her. He could not help admiring the splendid unconsciousness which the young girl showed. She did not even overdo; she was as natural as the waves lapping on the pier. She walked with a free swing; the light was in her hair again. They met; and he was going by!

" Good morning," she said vibrantly.

CHAPTER V

THEY spoke of the story in the *Eagle* office that afternoon. Donahue began it by complaining of the amount of space the city editor had given to the fire.

" What's the use of workin'? " he demanded, generally. " It all goes by favour."

" Donahue," remarked somebody, " is sore because McKinney caught him faking. He wrote up a big story, full of names and all, about a company that had been formed to build an artificial bog and furnish peat at low prices. He said the high price of coal was driving them to it. I heard McKinney asking him about it. ' What drove you to this, Joe?' he asked — ' the high price of whiskey?' "

" He gave the fire space because the story was worth it," some one else chimed in. " The story was a whale. I read it. Old Chambers did himself proud."

" It wasn't Chambers, it was Kent here,"

corrected two or three at once. The last speaker — Melton, the labour man — turned to look at Jerome.

"Well, it was good work, anyway," he retorted. Obviously the city editor shared Melton's feeling, for he despatched a note that day to Northrop.

"DR SIR,

"Some time ago you asked me to inform you, when I could fairly judge, whether Mr. Kent, the young man you recommended in May — would make a good newspaper man. I can safely say to-day that he will, if he wants to. The story of King & Co.'s fire, in to-day's issue of the *Eagle*, was his.

"Yrs truly,

"L. A. McKINNEY."

Furthermore, the city editor personally congratulated Jerome on his work.

"Not quite enough fireworks, that's all," he said. "You showed you had the powder, but you didn't light it all."

"Don't you ever believe in simplicity?" Jerome asked.

McKinney nodded. " If I was the owner of
the paper, why, yes. It would be my own
money I was losing then, and nobody but
me to kick. But I'm on a salary, you see,
and a man on a salary can't afford principles.
He's there to make money for the other fellow."

Another reporter overheard them.

" Don't pay any attention to him, Kent," he
advised. " Our worthy city editor has a theory
that he's a literary man and can give advice.
But don't mind him, and he won't hurt you a
bit."

" I keep my theories to play ·with, out of
business hours," retorted McKinney. " That's
more than you do, Chambers. Have you
finished those automobiles? Well, I've
got a little something for you to do in
the office."

" See what comes of helping others,"
groaned Chambers. He was small, alert, with
thick, dark hair; when he spoke, he had a
disconcerting habit of coming very close
and peering fixedly into the eyes of the
person he was addressing, as if he were
near-sighted. " See here," he continued,

"you live on Huron Street, don't you — at Kenealy's?"

"Yes," answered Jerome.

"I used to be there. Now I'm next door. Come round and see me to-night on your way home, won't you? I'm off early. I've got a pipe and some seven-year-old Castoria, and I guess I can find two glasses somewhere. Will you? Good again." He ran off.

In a few minutes a boy brought Jerome a note. He opened it.

"MY DEAR KENT,

"Haven't you neglected us rather shame-fully? Mrs. Northrop has been remarking that you have not paid your dinner call. Will you pay it this evening, at dinner? I am sorry not to give you more time, but Mrs. Northrop and my daughter go East to-morrow for the sum-mer. We dine at half-past seven.

"Faithfully yours,
"HENRY NORTHROP."

"There's an answer," said the boy. Jerome wrote: —

"Dear Mr. Northrop,

"Thank you very much. I will come, of course. It was extremely kind in you and Mrs. Northrop to think of me.

"Yours sincerely,

"Jerome Kent."

"I can drop around and see Chambers afterward," he thought.

"May I have the evening off, Mr. McKinney?" he asked later. "Mr. Northrop wants me to go to dinner to-night."

"Why, certainly," answered the city editor. He wondered what the relation was between the proprietor of the paper and this young reporter. He could not recall that exactly Kent's plea for an evening off had ever before been given in that office.

Jerome dressed for the dinner with care and trepidation. He thought of renting a dress suit, but sensibly decided that Northrop knew he possessed none, and was not asking him for his clothes, anyway. His trepidation, however, increased as he neared Northrop's house. He could have met the old gentleman with unmixed pleasure, but the prospect of another evening with women disconcerted him.   However, when he was fairly in, he found matters much easier than he had hoped for.   Judge Hetheridge was there, and a Miss Walton, a woman of perhaps thirty-five, with gray eyes and a pleasant mouth.

"I begin to suspect, Margaret, that the world is beginning to find out the concealment that has preyed upon my damask cheek," Hetheridge asserted when they were seated.   "This is the fourth time in two months that you and I have been next each other at dinner."

"The fifth, I think," Miss Walton returned. They began to count on their fingers.   "The fifth is right," she said.   "Judge, how could you forget the Martins?"

"Well," replied Hetheridge, defensively, "that wasn't a dinner, anyway, that was a lecture.   There was a long-haired fellow there," he explained, "who had the loudest voice of any of us; and when I tried to slip in something quietly to Margaret here, Mrs. Martin all but said 'Hush!'   He was a pet of hers from New York; some kind of a prophet, who had found a way to make money out of it."

Mrs. Northrop talked much, and frequently

to Jerome. " When we come back in the fall,
you must come and see us," she said. " I will
show you some nice girls, and some nice young
men, too. There are a number of splendid
girls who will be coming out this fall, I hear."

" Ethel Wheeler — Mr. Wheeler's daughter
— is coming out," Elsie put in, unexpectedly.
It was her first remark. " I saw Mary Strong
to-day. She knew Miss Wheeler at Pitthamp-
ton, and she told me. Mary says she is a great
beauty."

" Poor thing — what has she to come out
to?" lamented Mrs. Northrop. " What a pity
she should be so nice, when her father is such
a — "

" Now, now, Mrs. Northrop," Hetheridge
interrupted, lugubriously, " don't, I beg of you,
bring that man into the conversation, or Henry
here will leave us no peace until we have agreed
to rend the fellow limb from limb. Do you
know it is June, and yet nobody at this table
has said a word about golf? Heavens, suppose that should get out!"

" All the same," said little Mrs. Northrop,
" I think it is a pity."

When the ladies had gone out, Northrop re-
introduced the subject over the cigars.

" What do you think about his bill, Judge? "

Hetheridge shook his head. " Of course, he is log-rolling all the time. But he can't do anything definite for six months yet, when the legislature meets. I doubt if he gets it through. You knew he had pulled out of the Union Savings? "

" Yes."

" He has sold all his holdings. I hear from a friend of mine that he is speculating rather heavily in mines, too. I shouldn't wonder if he was getting old, Henry — like the rest of us."

" He could no more get old than the devil," replied Northrop.

" I believe you think he *is* the old gentleman," laughed the Judge, who had been serious for two minutes, and was tired of it.

" This young man here and Wheeler have a kind of a feud," remarked Northrop. Jerome looked at him imploringly.

" Yes? "

" Well, in a certain way. But perhaps I should not have spoken of it." He broke off, leaving Hetheridge with the impression of some mystery — the impression that piques curiosity. "Come, let us join the women folks." He led them in; he was not in evening dress to-night, as Jerome had gratefully noticed long before.

When they found the ladies, Mrs. Northrop was playing and Elsie was singing. She broke off at their approach, but Hetheridge took her hand and led her back to the piano. "I am an old man, Elsie, and a very bad one. Who knows whether or not I shall get to heaven? So you must sing for me here." She acquiesced calmly. Her singing, Jerome thought, he had never heard anything to equal. More colour came into her cheeks as she sang on. Presently her eyes met Jerome's, and they seemed to him to light like candles. He held his breath; he felt, somehow, as if she were singing to him alone. Even the Judge sat quietly. When she finished, she stood still a moment, her breast rising and falling, her face aglow. Suddenly it darkened, as if a mask had fallen. They made her sing again and again, and she sang magnificently, but not again did she reach that point of transfiguration. Jerome went away at eleven o'clock, having been offered a seat in Miss Walton's carriage. Elsie gave him her

hand, echoing her mother's wish that they
might see him in the fall. Her hand was, as
before, cool and firm, like a man's.

When Miss Walton set him down at the
corner of Rush and Huron streets, he had
promised to call and see her. He liked her
eyes and her quiet voice, a relief after Mrs.
Northrop's high pitch and the clamour of the
Judge. He stood still a moment on the corner.
The stars were out by myriads. Later he
found Chambers, in a gaudy bath-robe, hanging far out of his window to admire them.

" A fine show to-night," Chambers remarked.

" They're the only thing in Chicago that
makes me think of home."

" Where's home? "

" Scannell County, Indiana."

" Hoosier, eh! Well, here's something else
that will make you think of home." He poured
out a glassful. " Did your education include
the significance of the word ' when ' ? "

" We learn that in the primary school, in
Indiana," answered Jerome.

" Admirable system ! Teaches the essentials
first. Will you have a cigarette or a pipe? I

find my income does not permit of this luxu-
rious apartment and cigars also, but the others
I keep." He rattled on, a cheerful, slangy boy,
full of confidence in himself and of trust in
human nature. He spoke of the story of that
morning. "Where did you learn to sling
ink?" he remarked.

"I've been around a newspaper all my life —
a country weekly," answered Jerome.

"That's the place to practise. Now I
learned all I know at college, and that is, that
I don't know anything about it. I took all the
courses they would give me in composition out
there at the University, and when I got through
found I hadn't begun yet. The newspapers and
the colleges don't altogether agree on writing
English. College man?"

"No."

"Thought not. There are a good many in
the business, though; but not so many here as
in New York. Lots of 'em come on here right
from the high school, or even earlier; some of
'em begin as messenger boys and work up.
That's the best way, if you want to make a
good reporter, with a nose for news, so they
say. That means a nose a yard long, with a

hook on the end to stick into other people's business. The worse you write the better they like you, at first."

"I don't see that," interrupted Jerome.

"It's true, though. Every paper has its own style — picturesque like the *Eagle,* or suggestive like the *Eye,* or flip like the *Tomahawk.* If you have your own style, you see, you don't fit. Luckily for me I was university correspondent out at the U. of C. three years, so I learned. I sent them in accounts of everything that happened, and in dull times, of things that ought to have happened but didn't." He laughed. "They say the business is duller now, but in my day, three years ago, if the President sneezed it was good for half a column."

"Have you been on the *Eagle* three years?"

"Three years. That's a long time, in this business. There are mighty few men in the office who were there when I came. Three years on a newspaper is as long as ten years in business. They started me at fifteen dollars, jumped me to thirty dollars in a year, and there I've stuck ever since. They think it's good pay for a kid, and so it is, in a way, for I know two

I

or three fellows of my class at the U. that are getting a d——d sight less out of business than I am out of the *Eagle*. But then, they've got a future."

" Haven't we?"

" I'm blest if I know, Kent. When I came on I had the idea I'd be managing editor in five years. But I soon learned better. It isn't good writing they want of their managing editor, but a good head for business. They choose him in the same way Marshall Field picks a superintendent. They get a newspaper man if they can; if not, not. Now I'm looking for the dramatic critic business. I've written a few notices, when Hengle was off, and I like it. I like to go round and get drinks on Nat Goodwin and Henry E. Dixey, and a glass of milk with Mansfield. And I like to hear them all slash each other; nice as pie at first, you know, and then they'll let out a stinger from the shoulder. They're all for elevating the stage; but each one thinks, when you come to find out, that he has the only derrick in the business. Then I like to shake hands with Miss Terry and chin Sir Henry when he comes to town. They're a little offish, but bless their hearts, they know business is business; in the long run the box office manages them and the newspapers manage the box office. So they're pretty kind to us. So, as I say, I've got my eye out for dramatic critic. Just between you and me, old Hengle, our man, is going to New York pretty soon to look at an offer he's had down there from the *World*. If he takes it, that opens his place for me, do you see? They *may* get somebody else, but they'll have to go outside the staff to find him, and the old man won't do that if he can help it. Anyhow, they'll have to give me the job if they want to keep me. I've served my time reporting." He began to hum a verse from some negro melody — to the effect that without money one would find it useless to approach him. But an angry rapping on the adjoining wall subdued his singing. " I forgot it was after midnight," he apologized. " Have some more whiskey? " he peered into Jerome's face.

" Yes, thanks," Jerome pondered. " See here, Chambers, you said a minute ago you got fifteen dollars when you first came on. A week, or a month? "

" A week, of course."

"Well," remarked Jerome, defending his ignorance with a laugh, "they pay me by a thing they call space, and in five weeks I have earned just twenty-one dollars and sixty cents."

Chambers laughed. "That's the way they break a man in," he explained. "It's all over now, for you, probably. You'll find, Tuesday, that they've put you on salary. I hear they pay nearly everybody by space in New York, but much bigger wages. Dan Carey was getting twenty-five a week here, and went to double that in New York. He was back, stone-broke, in nine months. From which I conclude the pace in New York is about one minute and forty seconds to the mile. How's your ' nose for news ' ? "

"Short of a yard, I think."

" Perhaps you're like me; you can handle all the facts they'll give you and cry for more, but when it comes to hustling for them you prefer a day off — eh?   That's why I'm getting thirty a week instead of forty.   I'm the best man in the office, they say, at the fancy touches, but I do hate to hustle for details, and I guess they're on to me.

"It's a mighty funny thing," he went on,

" what odd ideas people generally have of newspaper work. I've an old aunt down in Milford, Illinois, where I come from, and I go down to see her now and then, so she knows I'm a newspaper man. But I believe a pile-driver couldn't push the idea out of her head that all I do is to stand on the corner and wait for something to happen. Now listen. About a year ago, there was a corking story broke loose out west of town. It was in a suburb crammed full of Dutchmen, all Kitwyks, and Vanderpoonders, and Maartens's, and the Lord knows what. One of those places you never see, you know, except from a car window, where you catch a glimpse of an old lady in short dresses on her knees weeding the cabbages. If you're with a girl, she probably says it's so picturesque, so exactly like Holland or France, and you can't think of anything but the cramps the old woman must have in her legs. Well, a tramp wandered into the place someway, and he insulted one of the women; tried to assault her; fact is, he did assault her. Those farmers got after him with pitchforks, and killed him there like a dog in the fields.

" We didn't hear of it, although it happened

along in the forenoon, until three o'clock —
the deadest, slackest time of day in the office.
Some Dutchman brighter than the rest just
happened to think of telling the police. I happened to be back, working on some fool thing,
when McKinney came rushing in. Lord, he
was excited! He rushed me and some others
down to the station; telephoned all round
town, found what men he could pick up, and
helped get a special train out right away. Half
the newspaper men in Chicago were on that
train or else came out hell-for-leather in whatever cabs they could pick up. We swarmed
over those market gardens like ants in the
sugar. They had fetched the body in, for the
woman to identify it, and there it lay in the yard
with a cloth over it, and flies thick on the cloth.

"Well, the Maartens and the rest of them
told me all they knew. We went over every
foot of those fields, saw where they had shot
him first, and then where they had finished him
with their forks, you know. I spent hours
hunting every detail of colour, and then I sat
down and wrote the lead. Oh, it was a daisy,
Kent. Here were the little plots of ground, all
green, and the stubby little houses, and the

people, half of them as Dutch as Flanders; and then here was the poor devil of a tramp, punched like a colander. It was easily the best thing I've done. Well, I sent it to my aunt, and what do you think she wrote back? She said I was lucky to have seen it all; and how did I happen to be there?"

"Complimentary to your style," put in Jerome.

"Best compliment I ever got; but think of the ignorance of it! It's characteristic. You find people howling at the reporters because they get things wrong sometimes. People forget the reporters have to find out from somebody else, and find out in a hurry. How can they tell a man's lying, or mistaken? The wonder is the papers are ever right."

"I've been wondering," Jerome remarked, "what takes people into this business of reporting — a love of adventure, or of writing, or what? I haven't made up my mind yet that I like it."

"Most of us drift in," said Chambers. "In a way reporting is a lazy man's job. It doesn't take any preliminary training, and it begins to bring in what lots of young fellows think is

good money, right away, so they take it up.
Most of the college men begin in the sporting
department, I guess. Oh, the whole thing is a
sort of bayou; they drift in and float around
awhile, and then probably they drift out again.
Few of them stay over five years. Maybe they
go into politics; maybe they're sent out to report some big bug's speeches, and make a hit
with him and get taken on as private secretary.
Maybe they have a chance in business. And
some of them go into literature. I remember
that Professor Edwards, at the University,
used to laugh when the men under him abused
the newspapers. All the young fellows who
teach English think the tip is to abuse the
papers. They hunt out all those icy construc-
tions that the best of us will slip on now and
then, and say, 'Look at the horrible writing!'
Of course, lots of it is horrible. But Edwards
was square. One day when I was talking with
him I told him I was going into the newspaper
business, and he laughed.

"'How about that *style* we've been trying
to nurse along,' he said. 'Aren't you afraid
the shock will kill it?' I told him I thought
I'd have to stand it, anyway. 'Well,' he said,

'maybe the heroic treatment will do it good.
You remember how the Spartans used to leave
their babies out over night on the mountain
sides naked? Some of them died, but the best
lived, and so the Spartans were a sturdy set,
on the whole. Perhaps,' he said, 'the newspapers are the mountains of literature.' Then
he spoke of a lot of men — Howells and Kip-
ling, and young fellows like Dicky Davis, and
Steve Crane, and Jesse Lynch Williams. ' All
newspaper men of one sort or another,' he said;
' some went to college and some didn't, but they
all lay for a while out on the mountain side.'
Have some more whiskey." He poured himself
a glass. " That was a great man, the governor of North Carolina," he added appreci-
atively as he drank. " I shouldn't wonder if it
was his name after all, not Toussaint L'Ouver-
ture's, that will be written in the clear blue
above them all.

" Well," he continued, " in case you are interested? All right. I drifted in, then, like
the rest. I was like three-fourths of the stu-
dents at the U., I had just about money enough
to squeeze through on. I played in the band,
and I sat in one of the libraries every day and

pretended to know where the books were, and
so with what I got from home I never ran out
of money. And I was always plugging along
with the English. I wrote stories by the hour,
all full of adverbs. I tell you I used to agonize
over those adverbs. When one of my girls
smiled, you'd better believe it wasn't just a
plain smile. It was more of a cocktail — if
you catch the allusion. It was always mixed
with an adverb. Maybe she smiled radiantly,
and maybe jocosely, and maybe seriously, and
maybe just pleasantly. I had my people analyzed down fine, always; but the beggars
would never do anything, or say anything
either.

" Finally, my senior year, I began to wonder
how about it. I'd always meant to be a lawyer.
You see my uncle was a minister and my
brother was a doctor, so I wasn't attracted to
those professions. But by that time I'd given
up the idea of being a lawyer, either; I'd as
soon be dead and buried as a young lawyer in
Chicago. I guess the sensations would be
about the same, anyway. Well, having nothing else to do, and no money to speak of, I
went on the *Eagle,* thinking perhaps I could

find out some things for my people — in the
stories, you know — to do. But I haven't
found them yet."

Here was a moment for confession! The
tribulations of his own people — in the story
— rose to Jerome's lips, but he kept them back.
Chambers's flood of revelation was very good
hearing, but he saw no reason why he, too,
should sit in the confessional. There was a
long pause.

"I hope you won't take offence if I say
something personal, Kent," remarked the other
man. "I take it we're about the same age and
we're going to live the same life for a while, so
I'll begin with a break. Why don't you buy
yourself a city suit?"

Jerome looked himself over. He was fresh
from Northrop's dinner, and yet this man evidently did not wholly approve of his appearance.
What, then, he wondered, had they thought at
the Northrops'. He was cut for a moment,
then he forced a laugh. "It's a matter of
money with me. No, I'm not offended."

"Money? It isn't the cost, Kent. I'm not
asking you to blow yourself for a P. A. or anything of the sort," replied Chambers, growing

more slangy under a slight feeling of embarrassment. "You can rig yourself up for
twenty-five plunks to the Queen's taste. You
ought to do it. You'll have some good big assignments now; I can see them coming in a
flock like blackbirds. Suppose you're sent out
to meet Lord Charles Beresford when he comes
through again; you don't want to go in hand-
me-down and a vest that shows two studs, the
way Donahue did; nor you don't want to cover
the flower show in overalls, either. Not that
I'm being personal, now; these are instances,
that's all. Just a knock-about suit that looks as
if you had been measured for it — you know?"
He found himself running on at length, and
was surprised. It was not Chambers's habit to
be embarrassed under any circumstances, least
of all, perhaps, when he was expounding to a
country cousin his chapter of the gospel of
clothes. But Kent generally possessed excellent control over his face — except when he
was talking to women. Chambers could guess
nothing of his feelings now, and was a bit put
out accordingly.

"Thank you," Jerome replied finally. "I
think you're right; I believe I'll do as you suggest."

" Good." Chambers was relieved. He was immensely taken by this countryman, and had not wished to spoil a possible friendship by an ill-judged impulse at its beginning. He felt himself also reinstated in the position of a guide. " This is a special matter. Of course on general principles the best thing to do is to save as much as you can. There's always a lady in the case after a while, and then it's good-by to the savings bank. I thank God she hasn't come to me yet. I guess I was vacci-nated so often out at the University that I'm immune."

Suddenly Jerome felt himself grow warm. By a tremendous effort he regained his self-control. He wondered if Chambers had no-ticed anything. Why under Heaven should he blush like a girl at the mere mention of one? He resolved not to be a fool.

" Well, good night," he said, getting up.

" Yes, the Castoria's out and it's one o'clock," answered Chambers, tipping the bot-tle. " By the way, Kent, what turned up to-night at the office? "

" I wasn't there," Jerome answered. " I went out to dinner — at Mr. Northrop's," he could not resist adding.

"What Northrop?" asked Chambers, idly, — "the old man?"

"Yes."

"The h——l you did," replied the reporter, with evident disbelief. "To meet the queen of England, or was it the Czar of Russia?"

"It was neither," Jerome retorted. "It was Judge Hetheridge."

"Is this the truth you're trying to tell?"

"Why, certainly. Good night."

"Good night." "And I sat here and told him he ought to buy some clothes," thought Chambers. *He* had never been asked to dine with Henry Northrop, and though he knew Judge Hetheridge, his was not by any means the knowledge of intimacy that is cultivated at little dinners. "Kent isn't proud, anyway," Chambers mused. "He sat here as if my whiskey was as good as the old man's must be. But I wonder who the lady in the case is?"

For Chambers had noticed the blush. It was his business to notice.

CHAPTER VI

A TRIFLE of wind stirred, but offshore, so that the lake was as quiet as a pond. Over at St. Jo, perhaps, the waters were running white, but by the sea-wall they lapped and rustled softly, as though the sun had turned them drowsy. Jerome Kent and the girl who had decided to come back into his life, loitered in the dreaminess of June.

He did not know her name; she had forbidden him to ask. "What's the use?" she laughed. "We have left out most of those formalities, haven't we? Let us leave out this one too. Of course you can find out easily who I am; but then you would show me, somehow, that you knew, and then I should not come here any more."

"I should not think of finding out, if you minded," he said, hurt, and showing it.

"Oh, no, no," she cried. "I know, I trust you not to try, you see — that is it, Sir Gala-

had. You don't mind if I call you Sir Galahad?"

"I like it," he answered simply.

"Do you know who he was?" She looked
at him inquisitively.

"Yes."

"What shall you call me?" she demanded
irrelevantly.

"Just 'you.'"

"Ah," she demurred, "that is too blunt."

"It is the only word I know that fits," he
laughed.

"Tell me," she asked suddenly, "did you
think it was odd I should speak to you again,
after what I said?"

"No," he answered, with evident truth. "I
had not fancied that you would, but it seemed
to me that you had a right to do what you
chose."

"Why?"

"Because you are a woman, I suppose."

She smiled. "That is a simple creed. Is it
really yours, or are you just saying so, as the
books do?"

"It is mine now, but I think I got it from
the books. Isn't it true? Don't you always do
what you please?"

"Oh, no!" she contradicted. "In the little things, the littlest of all, I do generally;
that is, I say what clothes I want, and where I
am to go for the summer, and things like that.
But in nothing else. See now: I am to come
out this fall. Mamma insists upon it; she insisted last year, but I wouldn't. Now I must.
I can scratch and bite and be disagreeable a
little while, but then I have to give in — just
like Speck when he takes his bath."

"How do you mean 'come out'?" he asked.
"Come out in society?"

"Yes. I am not old enough, really; or else
I am too old, I don't know. There is something wrong about me, I am sure."

"I am twenty-five," he confessed; "nearly
twenty-six. I am afraid I never came out at
all. Am I too old, or not old enough?"

"I don't know," she returned. "Could you
hold up a big bunch of pink roses and smile at
each one of your mother's friends as they came
up, even if you were so tired of smiling you
wanted to scream instead — but you don't
scream? Could you go out to dinner with boys
just back from college on their vacation, and
keep on smiling while they told you what clubs

K

they belonged to, and how Harvard had beaten
Yale — as if you cared! — and made jokes
about the champagne? Could you go to dances
afterward and talk about the floor and the
music, and how pretty you looked in pink, and
eat supper at midnight and come home at three,
and then do it all over again the next day, and
every day, till you almost believed in God because he sent Sundays to rest in? Could you
do that?"

"Oh, yes," answered Jerome, cheerfully.
"I could do that; I should like to."

"Well, then," she retorted disdainfully,
"you aren't too old to come out — or too
young. You're just the right age!"

"Don't you like it?"

"N-no. I don't know. I should, perhaps,
if the boys were the right boys, and the dances
were the right dances. But I don't believe so
— even then. I should like — " she paused.

"What should you like — most of all?" he
urged.

She walked on a few steps in silence. A
white gull, steering south, two or three hundred
feet out, suddenly shot downwards, so that the
sun glistened on his wings; then he steered up
again and sailed on.

"I suppose" — slowly — "to have wings like that gull, and fly away somewhere, where there was nothing to bother me — to see those elms and those violets, perhaps. Oh, you don't know; but I fell in love with those violets under the elms! What should you?"

"What should I like?" He hesitated. "I should like — most of all — to finish my book, and have it published."

"Oh, are you writing a book?" she cried. "Shall you put me in?" Then she blushed. "You know I didn't mean that."

"Very well," he answered tolerantly, "then I won't. But it's going to be hard to keep you out."

"Is it?" she flashed. "But you don't know me!"

"Ah, but then," he retorted, "you don't know my book!" They laughed together, because the June was bright, because the lake was gray-blue like snow, because they two were young; for any reason except his little inconsequential remark. Then she grew sober.

"I mustn't know who you are," she said. "But still you can tell me about the book. Is it your first? You're not Mr. Hamlin Garland?"

He was not, he assured her, Mr. Hamlin Garland. This was his first book. No one but he had ever seen a word of it — " nobody now living," he finished. She looked at him.

" My mother saw it," he answered the question she had not asked. " But she is dead."

" Ah!" She caught her breath. " I am — very sorry."

" You are sure," Jerome went on quickly, " that you won't go in the book?"

" How can I tell?" she cried. " I don't know what company I should have to keep!"

" The violets are in there," he said.

" What else?"

Then he told her the story of his book. It was no modern novel, with each character properly analyzed, and a neat little problem set out ready to be solved — the endless chain novel, which binds each author to find a new problem for every one he solves. It was a fine slashing romance of years ago, when the Indians overran the West as far as Pittsburg, and the settlers' only friends were axe and gun — a story of love and war, but more of war than love, as he realized when he retold it to this young girl. There were forays and ambushes, kind hearts and strong arms. "But it goes slowly," he said; "I have so little time."

She did not answer.

As the June wore on they had long talks together, morning after morning. Out of bits and scraps he pieced her life. She was evidently rich; she was fond of her father, who tried to give her everything in the world; she was too strong-willed and "queer" to please her mother, of whom she hardly ever spoke. She had been four years in a girls' school, and two summers abroad. She had few friends in the city, partly, he guessed, because she had been so much away, partly because she was thought to be a little odd. She admitted freely one day that people considered her rather unconventional.

"But they are wrong," she declared. "I am the properest of the proper — except when I can do as I please!" He dimly fancied, too, from the way she spoke of these "people" who surrounded her, that in spite of her wealth and beauty they built some barrier against her — though he could not guess what. He asked her, one day, to tell him of the interior of a particularly splendid and castellated structure, all

domes and peaks and towers, which threatened
the sun, within sight of them.

"Oh, I have never seen it!" she declared.
"I never shall see it, I suppose." She laughed,
and would not tell him why. He fancied a
trace of bitterness in her laughter.

"But aren't they a very fine folk who live
there?" he asked, half seriously.

"Very fine," she agreed. "Much too fine
for little me."

On his part he told her everything of his
life that seemed to interest her, and it was wonderful how interested she was, and how much
there was to tell. He was amazed to find his
own quiet existence had held so much of the
adventurous and the gay. When he spoke of
wide brown fields he had run barefooted
through, from April to November, her eyes
widened. "I always wanted to go barefooted," she sighed. "Sometimes I dream
that long ago, when I was a little, little girl, I
did. But I know that it was just a dream, and
I cannot do it any more." He told her how he
had fished and picked wild raspberries, until
the oil boom came, and civilization of the very
modern sort, which crowds out berry bushes

and kills all the fish; how later he had gone to
work in the printing office, and learned to set
type when he was twelve, and when he was
seventeen could get out the paper alone — his
father's paper, which his mother would never
sell, but kept for him through all the crowding
years.

"But I disappointed her — as I seem fated
to disappoint every one," he added sadly. "I
would rather write in the office than go out and
get the news, and so the paper didn't get on."
He told her of the first poem he had written, and
how he had set it up himself, and in the delight
of seeing the lines come out clear had printed
off fifty copies; and then how he had destroyed
all but two, one for himself and one for his
mother. "The poem was to her," he said.
He told how his mother failed slowly, and how
at last she died, and he sold the good-will and
the presses to the man who held the mortgage,
and came up to Chicago with a hundred and
twenty-five dollars, his unfinished story, and a
letter to a friend. Who the friend was, or
what he did, Jerome did not say.

"But," she questioned one day, when he had
been telling her of the long years through

which he had worked and written, " you never speak of any girl friends. Did you not know any women?"

"Oh, yes," he admitted, " I knew some."

" Tell me about them."

" Well — there was one, tall and dark, with splendid eyes. She was proud, and she had a temper, I think!" he laughed. " But I think I liked her best of all. You see I knew her from the time she was a tiny little girl. I am not sure that as she grew older I was not a little afraid of her, but I kept on liking her, because she was so kind, and fine, and lovely. I liked her — yes, I think I loved her." He stopped.

" What became of her?" the girl asked.

" She grew up and she married. Then — well, then I think she was very happy, but I am not sure. Her husband was not worthy of her." He stopped again. " But I hope she was happy. May I tell you her name?"

"Oh, no — never mind," she answered quickly; "I was only curious for an instant."

He went on without heeding. " Her name was Ethel."

"Ethel!" the girl cried involuntarily, "why!—"

"Yes?"

"Nothing," she returned, and bit her lip. "Ethel — what?"

"Ethel Newcome," he finished.

"Oh!" she cried again. "But she was a girl in a book!"

"Was she?" Jerome answered placidly. "Maybe so. But I loved her; and I loved more than any one else the man who introduced me to her — William Makepeace Thackeray, whom may God bless forever, Amen!"

"But had you no girl friends," she went on, "except in books?"

"No, not friends," he told her. "I have known very few other women than my mother."

"Perhaps," she exclaimed laughingly, "that is why you respect us so much. You have known so few!"

"I have been thinking," she told him one day, "that I never had a poem written to me. Write me a poem, Sir Galahad." It was when they had known one another a long time —

longer than Jerome's whole life before — that she said that. For three weeks he had been seeing her almost every morning.

"I should like to above all things," he declared. "Shall I write it now?"

"No," she commanded imperiously. "Talk to me now. But bring me the poem to-morrow."

He sat up late, when he came home from work, writing and thinking. Where was he drifting to? He had been, perhaps, barely conscious of drifting anywhere. And yet, though little learned in women or the habits of women, he was not a fool. He could not go day by day to the lake shore and meet this young girl, who laughed at him and commanded him and showed him moods as various as sunshine, without becoming aware that she liked him. And he? As he puzzled over his rhymes, the conviction began to grow up in him that his feeling for her was more than the liking for something in harmony with lake view and breeze and long June forenoon, with which he had begun. He knew when he ended his poem, that he, Jerome Kent, loved this girl, unknown to him by name, but known, he was sure, in all other ways. He did not know how easily any woman might have deceived him. He did not know that since the purity of his heart called out to purity, and that since in every woman, no matter how she may have trodden her soul in the mud, a spark of purity still burns, no woman *would* have deceived him. But this girl whom he saw like a jewel in every day's circle — that she was the diamond among women, he was sure as he had been of his mother's love — or, let us say now, of his own. That she was far more rich than he, he tranquilly accepted as a fact. That the handful called society would hold him no match for her, he knew. That he had never thought of marriage, or even of love, amused him. He loved her. Did she love him? He did not know; he hardly even cared, as yet. If he had searched his indifference to the bottom, he would have found it grounded on the unconscious conviction that she did. So he wrote his poem.

He carried it to her the next morning, but she seemed to have forgotten. There was a line in her forehead, which came sometimes when she was puzzled or annoyed.

"Why, do you think," she demanded, "is everything crossways in the world?"

"*Is* everything crossways?"

She nodded. "I have what the next girl wants, and she has what I want. It is as if we were all left-handed children, and God had given us all right-handed toys!"

"Oh, you can read plenty of essays on the philosophy of discontent," answered Jerome. "If we all had what we wanted, we should all sit still; who would there be to push?"

"I don't mean that," she declared slowly. "I understand ambition. I don't think I am ambitious, but I can understand it in other people. But when one hurts nobody, why should the world be so that one is hurt?"

"Why should children be unhappy?" he said. "Is that what you mean?"

"Children — or anybody. Sometimes I am a child and sometimes I am a woman, and I do not know which one is hurt worse. Now read me your poem."

"To the child, or to the woman?"

"To the child, Sir Galahad. It is always, I think, the child with you!"

He read it to her.

"The drums of the wind beat low,
   The hosts of the night are out;
I can see the flare of the stars
   Who have driven the day to rout.

"Thousands of years ago
   The torch of the furtherest whirled
To fling off the light that lies
   To-night on this little world.

"Thousands of years ago
   Ah, how straight and how far!
And love to the heart of a man
   Comes it otherwise, oh, my star?"

As he read the first two stanzas, she listened
with a critical interest, as yet, however, scarcely
comprehending. When he finished, he did not
at once look at her, or he would have seen her
lips part almost in a gasp. Who knows what
he might have said or done, if he had seen the
way she looked at him? But when he raised
his eyes, she was smiling contentedly.

"It is very pretty," she said. "Oh, yes, I
like it — though it seems a little academic
and stiff, don't you think? — a little bit of the
usual thing?"

He was chilled and puzzled. Had his mes-
sage been so direct that she was offended, or so

vague that she was unaware? What he had expected her to do he did not know, but not this. While he groped for the right words, she went on.

"I have only a minute this morning. Clothes, clothes! You see I shall be going out of the city soon. Indeed, I couldn't have come at all to-day if it hadn't been for the poem. Good-by."

"Till to-morrow, then," he answered, his brain still hesitant. Still she did not go.

"Well," she said, "aren't you going to give it to me, after all?"

Jerome's heart gave such a leap as he had never known. He handed her the paper silently.

"Thank you."

"You are not offended, then?" he asked hurriedly.

She looked at him, her eyes wide with surprise. "Offended? No, indeed. It is very pretty, really. Now good-by."

His heart sank again as he watched her go. She had not understood! Well, it was natural. He was a fool; how could she possibly guess that he had meant his poem in earnest —

he, unknown, to her unknown, and after little more than a double fortnight. Still she had taken the poem.

And she was saying under her breath as she hurried away, her eyes shining, " Sir Galahad! Ah, Sir Galahad! "

CHAPTER VII

IT was not until the next day that Jerome, in the turmoil of his brain over her reception of the poem, remembered another remark of hers — a passing phrase which seemed so imprinted on his brain, when he once recalled it, that he wondered how he had let it slip his thoughts a moment. " We shall soon be going away for the summer!" If he had needed any mark upon the bank before to show how far he had drifted, he had one now. The idea of spending day after day with never a glimpse of Her; the sounds of the whole city in his ears, and never a word of Hers — it was absurd and impossible. He hurried to the sea-wall to prove how absurd, impossible it was; and when he reached the place she was not there. He waited futilely throughout the morning; she did not come. Savagely he attacked his work in the afternoon and drove it through. He tormented himself with speculation. Had she

understood him and did not wish to understand? or had she really gone without a word?
or would she come again next day as she had
always done? They gave him an assignment
that took him far into the northwest part of
the city, where he had been on the first day.
He passed the John Kocynski School — the
second time he had seen it. The curtains were
drawn at the windows; summer had led the
children out of bondage. Jerome wondered
idly where the Jewish girl was who had given
him her address, "7777 West Adams — four
sevens." He made odd acquaintances, he
thought.

When he returned to the office he found a
note from Northrop asking him out to Lake
Forest over Sunday. "I have a special reason
besides the wish to see you," wrote the old man.
"Do not disappoint me." Jerome was to catch
the six-o'clock train. He was angry and disappointed. How could he go, when she might be
waiting for him the next day? And yet he
must. "I have a special reason." What reason? Ordinarily Jerome would have been
intensely interested in this mysterious phrase.
Now he speculated without heart. When, after

L

finding from McKinney that Northrop had arranged for his time off, Jerome caught the six-
o'clock train, he found the old gentleman, who
had discarded his heavy ulster, but still wore a
gray spring coat, leaning back in a seat all
alone.

"You see I managed to save one for you,"
Northrop said.

"Thank you," Jerome replied, almost curtly.
He was not in good humour yet. Northrop
watched him, as the young man sat squarely to
the front, moodily staring at nothing. He observed the wide-set brown eyes beneath the
broad forehead and the dark hair; he observed
the clean lines of the mouth, curving a little at
the corners; the strong shoulders under the un-
fashionable clothes. He thought, " He has the
power; has he the determination?" It was
debatable, perhaps, and yet Northrop wished
that he had such a son to carry on his work.
God had blessed him in his daughter, but his
name, that he had worked hard to make, must
die out.

"I never am really awake," he broke out abruptly, " until we pass Evanston; then I know
the city is only a bad dream, and life is real and

delightful after all. I have something to show you when we reach my place."

" The special reason you referred to, sir? "

" No, oh, no, that is entirely different." They lapsed again into silence for a while, busy each with his own thoughts.

" I hear that Chris Wheeler is dipping pretty heavily into speculation," Northrop remarked.

" Judge Hetheridge said something of the sort the other evening, I remember," Jerome added.

" Yes, I verified it. I make it my business to know as closely as I can what the man is at. He is gambling on a fairly large scale, nobody knows why."

" Perhaps he needs money now, to get more when his bill is passed."

" Possibly. I hope we shall disappoint him there. But I am inclined to think Hetheridge was right; the man is getting old and greedy. I have more hopes of beating him now than ever before. When a man begins on the stock market, especially so late as Wheeler has, he is on quicksands always. He can't give his best attention to his other affairs."

Northrop's trap waited for them at the station. When the old man was fairly seated he looked about restfully. The still woodsy town satisfied him.

"I love this place," he declared. The long June twilight hung about them as they drove amidst the groves. One bird, somewhere in the tops, was deceived into a sleepy singing, and they stopped to listen. The wind rustling from somewhere eastward fanned away the heat. Through long windows, deep set behind stretches of green lawn, they saw families sitting down to dinner. Northrop knew them all; here the Martins lived, here the Haywards, here the Hitchcocks. The old man's voice took on quietness as he pointed out everything. The shaded avenues followed no lines but their own sweet caprice.

At dinner Northrop spoke to Jerome of John Kent, his father.

"I met him thirty years ago," he said. "I suspect it was your father who put a purpose in me. I was always a dreamer of dreams; he made me wake. He had a kind of intensity of mind that was unusual, I think. I have seen many more successful men, but few who burned so. He had the consuming fire. I wonder if you have inherited it?"

Jerome remembered his keen, fierce, quivering little father; so quick, so unsystematic; so earnest and so tactless, so enthusiastic, visionary, downright, impracticable — his father, dead nearly twenty years. His father, like Northrop, had been a dreamer of dreams — of dreams in which he believed so passionately that they became the only realities. After all, what was a man with a purpose but a man who meant to make his dreams come true?

"I do not suppose," Northrop went on, watching the young man's face, "that your father would ever have been a great man. He lacked the money-making facility, for one thing; the world would not have known him. And then probably his intensity made him narrow. But what a patriot he could have made! what a martyr! Oh," he added suddenly, " Christopher Wheeler has much to answer for, but most of all that he killed your father!"

Jerome's revery broke in pieces.

" Killed him ? "

" Killed him, of course. Didn't you tell me as much? He is as responsible as any murderer ever is. And yet he has escaped all punishment. Poor John, poor John. Come," he added, " let us go into the garden."

The night had fallen when they went out. The old man led the way to a corner of the plot.

" Do you see these ? " He pointed to a number of bushes looming in the darkness. " Do you know what these are ? "

" I can't be sure," Jerome answered, peering; " but I think it is — "

" Hawthorn," cried Northrop, triumphantly. " I had them transplanted here, soon after you came. Do you remember how you told me you had walked unexpectedly by a bank of it ? These will bloom next year. I hope you will come out and help me enjoy them."

They went to church on the next day, at the hour when Jerome usually saw Her. Every one knew every one else. After the service, when he had met a few of the people who loitered out — among whom he was surprised to find Miss Walton — they dined in state. During the long meal there was still no word of the " special reason " which had brought the young reporter to Lake Forest. But after dinner Northrop led the way into the library.

"Let me see," he asked abruptly, "that paper you showed me once before — the one your father wrote before he died. Do you keep it about you?"

Jerome drew it out. "There, sir."

Northrop read it, puckering his brows. "I promise in the sight of God and man to devote my life to this one thing: I will see that Christopher Wheeler does as little harm in the world as possible. Jerome Kent. Your signature, you say?"

"Yes, sir."

"Well, my boy, what are you going to do about this?" The question was as sharp as a sword.

"To do?"

"Are you going to keep your promise?"

"How?"

Northrop laid a hand, white, thin, blue-veined, on Jerome's knee. The old man's eyes glittered like stars under his white eyebrows.

"This man killed your father. Many other things he has done, but this one comes home to you — he killed your father. That father you have promised — not to revenge, no; but to justify. As long as Christopher Wheeler re-

mains an unconvicted felon, your promise to
your father is not kept. Now listen. I have
found out from my superintendent that you are
a good writer and a clever man. I shall put
you on special duty on the *Eagle* — the duty
of justifying your father. This summer you
will train yourself for the work; and in December, when the legislature meets, you will go
down to Springfield as assistant to our political
reporter. There it will be your work to watch
what Wheeler and his agents do. We will
keep an eye on him up here. We shall know
where he goes and what he does there, and
sooner or later we shall find him doing something wrong. We shall defeat his bill; perhaps
we shall do more than that. It is quite within
the range of possibility that we shall find him
out utterly and send him behind bars. We will
league ourselves against evil as evil leagues itself against good, and by one means or another
we shall find him out!" His voice rose into a
cry. His eyes were like sparks on Jerome's
face. For the first time Jerome recalled Northrop's words of some weeks before — perhaps
this trailing of Wheeler was becoming a monomania with him.

"You have come at the nick of time," the old man went on more calmly. "I think Wheeler is failing; the luck is going to turn against him at last. He has done much harm while you were growing up to your father's wish, but we shall keep him from doing much more, you and I." His thin, delicate hand gripped Jerome's knee with a wonderful force. "You and I! You and I!"

But the young man was beginning to recover his wits, swept almost away in the suddenness of this onset. So the chance had come to fulfil his old promise! Did he wish to fulfil it? He thought of his book which he must abandon; the thought clutched his heart with an intensity perhaps hard to understand. He thought of the strain, the unpleasantness, of this life suddenly opened to him. Jerome was no Sybarite, but are there many of us to whom the existence of the detective appeals — after we have passed the boundaries of our sixteenth year? And this was the life of the detective, the life of the fanatic, the life of the blood-hound that offered. Yet — why had he come to Chicago? Why, in all these years, and against his mother's wish, nay, her command, had he kept that paper that rustled in the old man's hand now, like a live thing? He moved uneasily under the intensity of Northrop's look.

"I must sleep on this, Mr. Northrop," he said at last. "I must wait. I will answer you to-morrow."

"Can you doubt? Can you hesitate?" cried Northrop.

"Yes," replied Jerome. "This will rearrange my life. I must think."

"Very well," answered the old man, "think. First put that paper in your hand — so. It is your father speaking. Now — think!"

Jerome insisted on returning to Chicago that afternoon. The sight of Northrop's tired, keen old face had suddenly become an irritation to him. He could feel Northrop's eyes always upon him. He wanted to be alone. "I will tell you to-morrow," he repeated, and Northrop, against his will, was forced to yield. Jerome slept that night in his own room.

Or rather he did not sleep, until after two o'clock. When he rose and had breakfasted, he began to walk as usual toward the lake, revolving the matter in his mind. He thought constantly of Her, too. Had she gone vainly, yesterday, to the sea-wall, as he had gone the day before? Suddenly the promenade was before him — and there she was.

" Good morning! " He tried hard, but the joy was in his voice.

" Good morning, Sir Galahad." She was as gay as the breeze. Against her better judgment she had come, and she was glad.

They walked up and down by the lake, speaking of many things, infinitesimal things — the sunlight on the water, this world of eating and sleeping and drinking, and the city about them; but never of themselves. At last, however, by slow, even imperceptible degrees, they grew personal. And at length he opened his heart to her.

" What should you think," he said, " if I told you I had given up the book — for a while, at least? "

" Oh, no," she exclaimed. " You haven't! "

" Well, I don't know." He began to tell her the story of the promise he had made long ago.

" Once, years ago, my father and another man quarrelled. They were both in the wrong, perhaps, but the other man most. He was go-

ing to do something that would ruin many people — his friends. They quarrelled, and the
other man struck my father. My father was
not strong: he had a disease of the heart. The
shock killed him, of the quarrel, and the blow,
and all — not then, but six months later. He
made me promise, before he died, to do all I
could to keep the other man from ruining any
more people. But I was only eight years old;
I could do nothing!"

"Oh!" she breathed.

"Now — perhaps I can!"

Her face grew red, then pale. "You will!"
she cried. "Sir Galahad!"

"Oh," he answered moodily, "shall I? shall
I give up all my own self to be this thing, a detective? I must leave my book; I must leave
my leisure; I must leave all my likes, and take
up what I dislike!"

"That is fine," she cried. "It is like a Cru-
sade! Oh, if I were a man — I would help
you! This man — this other man — this
wicked man who killed your father; yes, yes,
you must keep him from hurting anybody else.
Think of having a purpose in life, something
grand to do! It is not revenge your father

wanted, I know, but to have you help other people. He is right, he is right! What is your book, when you can live? I am ashamed of you, Sir Galahad! Sir Galahad no more, unless you do this!" She had never been so roused, never so beautiful.

"But it is not certain that I shall succeed," he said, not yet convinced, or not willing to admit his conviction. "This other man is rich, he is powerful, he is unscrupulous, they say. I may give it all up and yet fail."

"Never mind," she exclaimed. "You will have tried, and you will not fail. Who is he, Sir Galahad, this other man?" Ah, that she might have guessed before!

"Christopher Wheeler," he said simply.

The training that a girl receives is perhaps the most wonderfully conceived of all educations in the world. It is in part the education of the connoisseur, and in part the training of the Indian: the cultivation of the nerves to receive the most poignant sensations of pain, and of the mind and muscles to hide their presence from the whole world. By that single name Ethel Wheeler's heart was turned to stone; her blood was ice in her veins; and yet, except for a sudden paleness of the lips and a sudden clasping of her fingers, she was as inexpressive as bronze.

"Oh!" was all she said.

"I think," he went on, "I think — I hope — I should succeed. But I may fail."

She wondered how long the pain would last. "I hope," she replied steadily, "that you will choose — for the best. And now good-by, Sir — " She stopped midway of the half-mocking title she had used so often.

"Good-by?" he demanded. "Why — what?"

"I am going away," she said, "to-morrow."

He stood still. "For how long?"

"Oh," she answered lightly, "always, I think."

"Always!"

"Good-by," she said again. Oh, if he would but go and leave her alone!

"But — but — " He did not move.

"This has been very romantic, hasn't it?" she said. Her voice was level; she spoke very rapidly and did not look at him. "You see, I always wanted to know a man as he really was; not the conventional kind of a man who com-

pliments you all the time, but a man. So I
have liked to know you, Sir — " She broke
down upon the name once more, but hurried on. " You have been very good to me;
you haven't taken advantage — of my speaking
— in this — way. So, now, good-by. Oh, *do*
go!" she cried. Her whole heart was in the
word.

But he only moved closer. " And I? How
do you think I am to endure — this?" he half
whispered. " I have taken no advantage; but
have you given me no rights? You know —
we both know! When I came here this morning I meant to tell you I loved you. I tell you
now — I love you, I love you, I love you! I
am Jerome Kent. That is all I have to tell you
— just my name. The rest of me you know.
Tell me this, before you go — do you love me?
You have let me love you — Ah, that you must
have known! Do you love me?"

The world seemed to be whirling about her.
" Oh, no, no, no!" she cried. " Please, please
go! Oh, how could you — how could we —
oh, my poor, poor father!"

He had no understanding; but he saw now
that she was in strong distress. " I will go!"

he answered. " But I am absolved from what
I promised you. I will not let you out of my
life. I will find out who you are, and come
then and tell you again what I tell you now —
I love you and I always shall! "

" Ah, if you *should* come! " she sobbed.
" Promise me," she asked wildly, " that you
never will; that you will never try to find out
who I am! "

" I know now," he answered stubbornly.

" You know! "

" No — not your name, nor where you live.
But I know who you are — you are the girl I
love! "

He left her and strode down the walk, while
she cried silently.

" Oh, Sir Galahad! Oh, Sir Galahad! " she
wept.

CHAPTER VIII

JEROME's interview with Northrop on the same day was sharp and decisive.

"You will take the chance, then?" the old man said.

"Yes."

"You are wise," commented Northrop. "I thought so."

The reasons which led Jerome to accept the new place were simple. He would almost certainly have taken it in any case. The meeting by the lake decided him finally. What he wanted now was work. He wanted it feverishly. And yet he was not wholly disheartened by what she had said. He had demanded whether she loved him, and she answered no, it is true; but why, if she did not care, had she been so troubled when she went away? Jerome's feelings moulded themselves into a fierce determination that startled him — an intensity which might have been the direct inher-

itance of his father. He would become more
than Jerome Kent, reporter; then he would see
her again. To his end this was the first step.
He was not blind to the advantages of securing
Northrop's interest.

On Tuesday, as usual, his weekly check was
handed him when he passed the cashier's desk.
He looked at it idly — twenty dollars. Chambers, then, was right, and he had been put upon
a salary at last; and he was pleased in spite of
himself, although events in the last few days
had so whirled him along that the check
seemed a very small matter now. He had at
least, in his first effort, made a good beginning,
he thought, remembering that Chambers began
his servitude at fifteen dollars.

As the days went by, life took on its old routine. His ideas about abandoning his book, he
found, were mock heroics; he still had his day
off, when he might have worked. But he seldom did. He preferred, in his restlessness, long
walks about the city, among the poor and the
rich, in which he watched always — for what?
He could hardly have told. Certainly not for
Her; she was gone away, she had told him.
Perhaps he watched for remembrance. He

found out much about the young, busy, un-
washed, giant of a town, which has so little
right yet to call itself a city among cities, unless
impudence gives the claim of age, but will not
wait for the praises that energy is sure to win
some time.   The training that Northrop had
mentioned was already begun.   The office put
him on political assignments, sometimes alone,
more often with Hanlon, the political editor —
to interview the mayor, or the acting-mayor
when the mayor was gone fishing, as he generally was; or to find out, perhaps, what the
chances were for the Associated Charities Bill
when the Assembly met; or to pick up a little
preliminary gossip on the coming contest for
the speakership — for the speaker of the previous half of the session had died in May.   It
was a dull season, this summer; an off-year,
they called it.   But he came to know Arkell,
and Laramie, who were Wheeler's chief aides-
de-camp in the legislature; and to find out a
little of the peculiar motion with which the
wheels of politics revolve.   He had been at
this work for a month, and was settling into
the grooves, when chance, which had let him
be for a while, suddenly noticed him once more.

The drama began in the office, to which Jerome returned about half-past ten o'clock of a hot night in July. If all that July had not been heated like a furnace, one might have supposed the night a weather-breeder, as the New England word has it. McKinney seized upon him when he appeared.

"See here, Kent," he asked, "go with Chambers out on the West side, will you? I've just heard from White, who's doing police there, that a story has broken loose on Adams Street — a girl shot herself, or something. It may be good, and in that case we shall want the story in a hurry; so I'd like to have the two of you there."

"I've just come back from 64th Street," Jerome answered.

"Never mind," Chambers cut in, "come along. Ten to one it's only the old story, and we have our cab ride for nothing. Besides, it's not far."

"Where is it?"

"7777," replied Chambers.

"What?" The number awoke a reminiscence in Jerome's brain, and he laughed. "I'll go, of course."

"I've been — what do you think?" Chambers demanded when they were reclining in their cab. "Hustling the hotels for tips — no less. Trying to scare up some sort of news somewhere. This is the dullest summer in years. Well, I prefer cab riding."

When they reached 7777 they found a small crowd gathered before it, talking loudly.

"That's the window, the one there with the green blind." "No it ain't; it's the one where the curtains is down." "I seen her come out of here yistiddy; you'd 'a' thought she owned the town, then." "Look at them fellows goin' in." "Nawthin' but reporters on some paper."

A woman, answering the bell at last, nervously peered into their faces. Chambers explained who they were.

"Oh, well, I s'pose you'll have to come in," she interrupted. They entered, and she shut the door quickly, with an angry glance at the crowd below. "Oh, yes, she killed herself. You can see her, I s'pose, if you want teh." Her voice shook. "Pretty reputation it'll give my house to have ever'body know they'se a person died here! Seems as if ever'thing was against a woman!"

She led the way upstairs, her voice, lamenting, clamorous in the still house. " Will any more of you men be coming? There was another here just a few minutes ago. I declare it's a shame to try and spoil folks' business, putting things in the papers about their house. I'd 'a' had this girl out in two days, too!" She threw open a door. " Here — she's in here."

" Hush!" said some one within. A girl rose from a chair by the bed, hesitating, shaking. " Oh, Mrs. Haines, don't!" Her voice trembled with fright.

" Why, Miss Wilcox, what you doin' here?" the landlady demanded, shocked.

" Oh, I couldn't leave her all alone! She never liked to be left alone!" The girl swayed, and would have fallen if Chambers had not caught her in his arms.

" You see," cried Mrs. Haines, with triumph in her voice, "I told you how it would be. You ought to have stayed away as I told you."

The girl shivered.

It was a mean room, whose tasteless wallpaper and cheap carpet defied some feminine attempts at adornment — the lithographs, the muslin curtains, the artificial flowers upon the mantelpiece. A trunk, open, half packed, stood in one corner, by a thin curtain which swayed in some invisible draught, and caught grotesque shadows from the lamp upon the table; a dress or two, hanging behind it, were startlingly resemblant of human figures. For a moment Jerome fancied the woman must have hanged herself there. Then Mrs. Haines turned. Jerome followed her eyes. To him it seemed the added touch of horror that the dead woman should be lying on a folding bed.

He went up to the body. He had seen death too seldom to lose the awe it gives. It is so common a thing, death, that we speak of it without hesitation or fear. Yet, to most of us, when we see the dead face to face, the mystery and magic of the word returns — death! the easiest, the most awful of all things. We have all quoted the marvellous phrase of Hamlet — " from whose bourne no traveller returns." It is only as we see the traveller, gone upon his journey, that we have an inkling of the phrase's meaning. So with Jerome.

" I thought she shot herself? " he said, under his breath.

" No — poison," the landlady answered with a sniff. " There's the bottle on the mantel. I took it off the bed."

Jerome bent over. A faint sweetish, sickish odour was in his nostrils. The woman's night-dress lay open at her throat. She was Jewish, and had been pretty. Above her right eye appeared a little scar, like a heart. He felt very sick. It was for this she had given him her name and her address, the girl at the John Kocynski School.

" Why did she do it? "

The landlady stared. Chambers, who had followed to the bed, put his hand on Jerome's arm and looked around quickly for little Miss Wilcox; but she had her arm over her eyes, crying quietly, and did not notice. " That girl oughtn't to be here," he insisted abruptly in a low tone. " Find out what you can, while I take care of her." Chambers went up to Miss Wilcox and touched her gently on the shoulder. " You mustn't do this," he said, " you will be sick. Let me take you out."

" Oh, I can't, I can't! " she cried. " You will leave her alone! She never wanted to be left alone! "

"You must," he said sternly. "I promise you she shall not be left alone. Come." She looked up at him, her breast heaving; he kept his eyes on hers, and in a moment she rose submissively and followed him out.

"Well, ain't you most through?" questioned Mrs. Haines, querulously.

"Her name?" Jerome asked, hesitating.

"Goldberg—Etta Goldberg." Mrs. Haines mingled her information with her laments. Yes, the girl was a teacher, or had been. She'd had a good deal of money, a time back, apparently; paid her board regular. "But Monday I told her she was to pack. I was goin' to put her right out Friday, but she said her money was gone, and she begged, so I let her stay. An' *this* is what she does for me," concluded Mrs. Haines. "How'm I going to let this room, I'd like to know? Oh, you can say people won't know, but they find it out. D'you think anybody wants to sleep in them sheets?"

"You say she had no money," Jerome went on. "That was why she killed herself, then?"

Mrs. Haines laughed harshly. "D'you say you're a reporter?" she asked. "Yes; that was why."

He would have pressed her further, but at that moment a heavy wagon, driving up with a rattle, stopped before the house.

"It's the police, at last," she announced, going to the door. "Well, it's about time they came." Jerome, looking by the curtain, saw that a yet larger crowd had collected about the ambulance. Two big blue-uniformed Irishmen pounded upstairs, eyed him closely, and then wrapped the dead woman in a quilt. One of them bore it downstairs like a baby; the quilt trailed between his feet so that he swore. Yet he was not rough; he stepped carefully, if heavily; and he had stopped to cover the face.

Chambers joined Jerome in the hall, and they followed the policemen out.

"Did you get the details?"

"I think so," answered Jerome. "I don't know."

"I know how you feel, old man. New to you, isn't it? Having the other little girl there made it worse, of course — and then the Haines woman. She was pretty, don't you think?"

"Yes — she had been."

"Of course you hardly had a chance to see

her. But I could tell that when she hadn't been crying she was pretty — especially her eyes."

" Crying? " Jerome stared. " What are you talking about? "

" Why, about the little girl — Miss Wilcox."

" Oh! " answered Jerome. " I meant the other one." They were silent awhile.

" Well," remarked Chambers, finally, " it's as I thought; we've had our cab ride for nothing, and that's all."

" What do you mean? "

Chambers lit another cigarette. " No story there, of course; two sticks, maybe, but I doubt it. It happens every day."

" I'm not sure yet why she killed herself," pondered Jerome. " Of course — "

" Couldn't you *see?* " interrupted Chambers. " Ah! "

" Oh, the world is full of brutes," commented Chambers, cynically. " Wait for me while I write this, will you? "

" If you don't mind, old man," Jerome answered, " I won't. I'm a little upset, and I'm going to walk around awhile."

" All right," replied Chambers, sympathet-
ically.

The thought of his room made Jerome restless. He was too hot and too disturbed to
sleep. He walked north, toward the sea-wall.
The moon was dead, and the stars gave little
light on the quiet and solitary streets. When
he reached the lake he stood wondering for
some time. Where was She, who had walked
with him there so often, and when should he
see her again? After a while he turned back.

On his way home his steps led him by
Wheeler's house. The misshapen mansion
sprawled on one of those short side streets between State and the lake, whose topography is
best known by grocery wagons and the coach-
men of the rich. It was after midnight, and
there was no light about the place, which
bulked dimly among its neighbours. Jerome
leaned against the iron fence and contemplated
the house. There lay the man whom he was
to oppose all his life long. The man had never
heard of him; would not care if he did hear.
A little of the excitement of chase crept into
Jerome's heart. It was odd that in all his restless imaginings — and he lived for more than

half his life in his mind — the thought of
Wheeler as a *man* had never come to him.
The banker — banker no longer now — was a
presence, a sort of embodied villany he was to
overcome, if he could.   He felt no animosity
against him.

As he leaned there, watching the quiet house,
some one, somewhere, cried "Help!" — a
man's voice, half muffled.   Jerome listened in-
tently.   There was nothing more.   He began
to run as hard as he could toward the place
whence he fancied the sound.   Suddenly he
turned a corner, and in the darkness could just
make out two men bending over a third.   They
ran at his quick footsteps; he pursued a little
way and then returned.   As he stooped to pick
the figure up, the man stirred and groaned.
Then he sat up, and his eyes fell upon Jerome.

"Ah, *would* you!" he said thickly.

"What's been happening?   Are you hurt?"
demanded Jerome.   The man put his hand to
his head, and took it away stupidly.

"Hey?"

"Can you get up?"   He tried to help the
other to his feet; after a struggle the man was
up.   He was very large, ponderous in every

limb. The light from a street lamp fifty feet away fell upon his bleeding face. It was Christopher Wheeler.

"Held up, by G——d," he said. "Held up on my own doorstep." He seemed to understand now that Jerome had come like the good Samaritan, and he was disposed to take advantage of the opportunity. He put his hand on Jerome's shoulder.

"Take me home, young man," he said. "You'll not lose by it. They hit me on the head," he explained. "They'd have done for me, if I'd been any other man. But Chris is too tough for any of 'em." He mumbled to himself, his brain apparently upset by the shock. "Blood all over me!" he cried suddenly. He was nearly right.

The two held a fairly steady course for Wheeler's house, though the old man stumbled frequently, and clutched at Jerome for support. When they reached the door Jerome would have rung, but Wheeler prevented him.

"No — this way," he said, fumbling for his latch-key.

"But you will want help," Jerome protested. "The servants."

"To h——l with 'em," replied the old man. "What's your name?"

"Never mind," answered Jerome. "Call me Smith."

"'s that your name?"

"Maybe. I'll say good night now, Mr. Wheeler. But you'd better let me ring for the servants."

"Here," said Wheeler, imperiously. He was still fumbling helplessly for his pocket-book when Jerome passed out of sight. At length he desisted, and stared into the darkness. "Gone!" he thought. "That was one of 'em, I'll bet." He staggered to the steps, for physically no braver man existed than Christopher Wheeler. He meant pursuit. But at once he realized the futility of it. It was by an effort only that he got into the house.

Meanwhile the unconscious Jerome passed the scene of the robbery. He stood there a few minutes, thinking of the encounter. "It's a pity they didn't hit him harder," he thought, "and end it all." Then he walked on. As he passed under the street lamp something on the sidewalk caught his eye, and he picked it up. An open pocket-book! He examined it hastily

by the lamplight. There was nothing there;
the pocket-book was empty. He took a few
steps toward Wheeler's house and then he
paused, struck for the first time by the fact that
this robbery was news, and if he was quick the
Eagle could make a " scoop." Looking at his
watch he found it was nearly one o'clock, and
he began to run toward the office. He could return the pocket-book in the morning.

When he reached the office, Adams, the night
city editor, asked at once, —

" What's up? "

" Christopher Wheeler was held up half an
hour ago in front of his own house."

" Sure? "

" I got there a minute later."

" Who was with you? "

" Nobody."

" Old man hurt? "

" Quite a goodish bit."

" Is it a scoop? "

" It surely is," laughed Jerome, " unless the
boys that held him up were reporters. There
was nobody else there."

" Rush it through," commanded Adams.
" Give it half a column." He whistled through

a tube. " Oh, Mac! Kill that dog story for
the second edition; I've got something better.
John," he cried to the office boy, " look up that
double column cut of Wheeler." Jerome was
already deep in his story. They took it page
by page as he wrote it. When he finished the
fifth the first had been long in type. He went
for a sandwich and a cup of coffee at half-past
two, and by the time he had finished, the great
presses were clattering off thousands of copies
of

" BOSS " WHEELER HELD UP.
THE PROPRIETOR OF UNION GAS
BEATEN AND ROBBED ON HIS
DOORSTEP.
THIEVES   ESCAPE   WITH   THEIR
PLUNDER.

By the time that Christopher Wheeler had sunk
into an uneasy sleep, the early birds in their
night-shelters were reading of his misadven-
ture.

The scamper of his effort to get his news in
print kept Jerome thoroughly awake. When
he reached his room the dawn was stealing into
the window, but he was not sleepy yet. He
lighted the gas and drew out Wheeler's pocket-

N

book. It was bulky, red and coarse-grained, opulent and imposing — like its owner. As he observed it, Jerome noticed what had before escaped him — two or three compartments still unopened. He looked in one — no money, but papers. And then a strong temptation assailed him — to examine these papers which fate had tossed in his way.

The revulsion against the idea came almost simultaneously. That would be a detective's work indeed. And yet — How far was he bound by the promise he had made to Northrop, and, further back, by the promise he had made to his father? What would his father or Northrop do, if chance threw in their way an opportunity like this? He did not need to ask the question. But they were fanatics, he thought. Should he be a fanatic too? Certainly to examine this pocket-book would be a sneaking thing to do — like opening a man's mail. Suppose, as was wholly probable, there was nothing of importance in it, he would part with his own self-respect and get nothing in return; Esau and the mess of pottage. On the other hand, had he the right to let the opportunity slip? An easy way out would be to

keep the pocket-book intact and carry it to Northrop in the morning, leaving the burden of the
decision with him. But that would be to decide
himself, nevertheless. Jerome was sure Northrop would look the thing over. Northrop
had called him " Hamlet " two months before.
Was he such a man, hesitating, indecisive?
With a sudden resolution he spread the papers
out on the table. Out of the mists of the past
he had seen his father's face, keen, thin, determined, a man who might be right or wrong,
but who could choose, at least, a path for himself, and follow it, a man who could shut his
eyes to the technicalities of honour when he was
doing what he conceived to be his duty. Jerome took the old, yellowish, written promise
out, and laid it on the table, to strengthen his
own determination.

The papers seemed after all to be nothing of
importance. The first was covered with figures in a careless hand. There was not a word
on it; he thankfully laid it aside. The second
was a memorandum of engagements, half intel-
ligible; names upon it that we all know and
names never heard of — politicians, merchants,
nobodies. There was material in it, perhaps,

for a dozen romances, but nothing to reveal Wheeler's acts, and he laid that aside also. The third and fourth were letters which he read conscientiously through. They confirmed Northrop's statement that Wheeler was specu-lating — that was all. He put them aside. The fifth, he saw with a feeling of relief, was the last. He unfolded it — only a list of names. They were alphabetically arranged, he noted, beginning with Acker and ending with Wilcox; there were many between, written very small and close together in a thin, fine hand. Then he observed that each name bore a note, in a different hand from the body of the writing. Most were merely " O. K." or " N. G."; but in many cases there were figures, from 500 up, written thus: 500(?). The whole list puzzled him. Then, as he began to read the names, a light came to him. Here, far up on the list, was Arkell — he knew that name. " O. K." was opposite it. Jerome searched among the Ls. There was Laramie, as he had expected — also " O. K.'d." He looked for Morton, and Wellington, and Powelton — all names he knew — and found them. He knew now that this was a list of the members of the state legislature, annotated in the handwriting of Wheeler.

Abruptly he tossed the paper back upon the table, and went to bed. This might mean something or nothing, but at least he was sick of the whole matter. He had committed himself now. In the morning he would carry the affair to Northrop and turn over the responsibility. He slept, after a time. In the morning, as he planned, he took the pocket-book to Northrop. The old man seized upon the list like a hawk. The same extraordinary fierceness was in his eyes as had shone there when he bound Jerome to keep his old promise.

" Of course," he cried, " this is important." He demanded the story of how Jerome had come by it, and listened eagerly. He called up Hanlon, the political editor.

(This man needs, perhaps, some introduction. He was a Chicagoan when he was christened James Joseph Hanlon. He had received his education in Chicago; he expected to die in Chicago. He had come on the *Eagle* as messenger boy, and when he speedily earned the distinction of being the only boy on the paper who never needed to be sent back to correct

mistakes, he was transferred to the reporters'
room.   There in a short time he was detailed
to assist the "city hall man."   He was then
twenty-one.   At twenty-five Mr. James Hanlon, city hall man, was one day called into the
office of the managing editor.   He impercept-
ibly adjusted his tie, flicked imaginary dust
from his coat sleeve, and responded.

"You know, Mr. Hanlon," said the managing editor, formally, "that our political man is
leaving us.   We hope that you will take up his
work on Monday.   The salary will be sixty-five
dollars a week."

"Thank you, Mr. Latham," answered Hanlon.   "But I am afraid I can't do that."

"Why not?"

"The *Eagle* is Republican.   I am a Democrat."

"Why, you harebrained Irishman," snarled
the managing editor, "will being a Democrat
keep you from getting the news?"

"Not at all."

"Then get it — and we'll attend to the pol-
icy at this end.   Is that satisfactory?"

"Quite so, Mr. Latham."   He bowed and
went out.   The managing editor turned to his
secretary.

" One of us two," he remarked, looking after
Hanlon, " was born in Boston and got a degree
from Harvard College; and one was born on
Blue Island Avenue, and got a degree from
the West Division High School. But which,
Frank?" The secretary wisely refrained from
answering.)

Mr. Hanlon found the proprietor of the
Eagle in company with Kent. " What's up? "
he wondered; but he said nothing.

" Read that." Northrop thrust the list at
him.

" List of the state legislature," answered
Hanlon, in a moment.

" Anything else? "

" Well, Mr. Northrop," he answered deliberately, " it looks like a kind of prophecy about
the attitude of the different members on some
question."

" Do you know the handwriting those notes
are in? "

" No, sir."

" It is Christopher Wheeler's. Compare it
with these."

Hanlon did so, his eyes lighting. " It is his,
no doubt," he replied presently. " Mr. Nor-

throp, this is very valuable. May I ask where you got it?"

"Kent found it." Northrop told the story, which Hanlon received impassively. He had read in the *Eagle* that morning of Wheeler's robbery. He knew, though vaguely, that Kent was detailed to assist him, particularly in the Wheeler case. Now he was wondering at the boldness with which Kent put forward this flimsy tale to account for the possession of the pocket-book. He admired the nerve which would go to any lengths, even of assault, possible murder, in the good cause. But he thought young Kent ought to invent a better yarn.

"Well," he said, "this is very important. Now what I should do is this — keep it dark for the present; destroy that pocket-book, or hold it, at least, and say nothing. Meanwhile, have a full-page facsimile made of this list. You see, it's worth absolutely nothing in a court. It's no evidence at all — just a few figures. But hold it till the legislature meets; hold it till everything's on a strain; the public excited over the gas-bills, and the legislature on the *qui vive* to find who is crooked — if anybody is. Then publish your facsimile. Do you think there is one of these men marked with figures who won't squirm out of voting for the bill? It would be as much as their life is worth, some of them. More than that — they'll see how each one is rated. Of course you understand these amounts don't stand for so much money paid over. But they give a basis of comparison anyway. The little fellows will want more, but it will be too late then; and they'll change their votes out of spite, if they wouldn't for their constituents. Between this thing and that thing, the facsimile, if we bring it out at the right time, will kill that bill and bury it miles deep."

" But isn't it possible," demanded Northrop, his eyes devouring the paper, " to indict — using this as a basis? "

" No, sir. You might consult a lawyer, if you want. But it's waste paper, if you try to use it that way."

When Hanlon had gone, Northrop turned to Jerome.

" I shall destroy the pocket-book," he said, almost in a whisper. " It might turn up at any time, and spoil our plan." His fingers, thinner

than ever, worked nervously. "Is it empty?"
He pulled it open once more, searching every
nook in it. Suddenly he came upon still another compartment, cunningly hidden in one
cover. "Ah!" He had something. His fine,
delicate old face sharpened as he drew it out.
But it was only a small photograph of a girl.
"'Ethel!'" he read on the back. "'To my
dear father!' Poor girl, poor girl! By God's
grace, my dear, we'll destroy some of your
father's schemes now!"

"Let me see it, please," asked Jerome.
What was the daughter of this man like? Northrop handed it to him, and he saw Her.

"I must have this," he said at last, with an
effort. "Treasure-trove."

"Better destroy it," counselled the old man,
keenly. But Jerome took it away.

When he had gone Northrop burnt the papers and the pocket-book in the grate, with a
smell of charring leather. The room was already warm, but he hung over the little blaze
with his hands to it. Then he spread the list
out on his desk and examined it for a long
time. His enemy — for such he had grown to
feel that Wheeler was — lay in his hands;

they were tense to seize their prey. He sat so long without ringing his bell that the watchful Robert, without, dominating the roomful of those who waited, grew fearful of something wrong, and — for the first time in his life — opened the door before the summons came. Northrop was sitting still at his desk, his eyes glowing as he turned his head. Robert hastily drew back.

"Is dere sumfin gone wrong with Mistah Northrop?" he speculated. But in a few moments the little bell of the private office rang as usual, and the stream of callers began to flow once more.

CHAPTER IX

THE summer waned; the scorching July was
followed by a cool August, in which the city's
fifteen thousand who do not go to the mountains or the seashore rejoiced, and the newspapers bragged of Chicago as a " Resort."
Jerome worked hard, even fiercely. There was
nothing to do, and yet some devil was in him,
driving him on. When he had taken the little
picture home he had placed it on his table and
stared at it a long time, seeing more than the
graceful turn of the head, the clear eyes, and the
strong lines of the mouth. He saw a girl in
white, who told him she loved the violets that *he*
had spoken of; who knew his heart, all of it —
and knew that it was hers. He saw her again,
and she was running like a child, her face gay
with laughter. He saw her again, and she was
crying as though her heart would break. Then
he saw her no more, but put his face down on
his arms. When he rose, he put the picture

away.   Never, during all the months, did he
look at it again.

Late in August Chambers came into his
room one night when they had walked up from
the office together.   Since Jerome had taken
Chambers's advice about the clothes, that eager
journalist had regarded himself as the mentor
regularly appointed of this big, quiet young
man, whom in the warmth of his heart he soon
began to love like a brother.   He deluged Jerome with advice in season and out of season
— advice on work, advice on recreation, on
how to spend his money and how to save it,
on women, on politics, and on art.   He was so
happy in giving it and so pleased when any
of it was carried into action by Jerome, that
to the latter Chambers was the single spot of
brightness in the dreary days.   But to-night
the young reporter seemed moody; his cheerful rattling talk was subdued into abstraction.

" Did you ever think, Kent," he asked at
length, " what a devil of a poor excuse a boarding house is for a home? "

" Did you ever think," Jerome responded,
" how poor we devils are who live in them? "

" Not so poor," Chambers retorted with

spirit. "I'm getting thirty a week; that's fifteen hundred a year. You're drawing twenty-five, aren't you? that's twelve-fifty. There's many and many a boy in Chicago who would be in heaven to draw half as much as either of us."

"If you drew half as much," Jerome answered idly, "with your ideas in food and drink, Will, heaven would be the only place for you. You couldn't live on earth."

"Now come off," Chambers cried. "I save regularly."

"How much?"

"Five dollars a week," admitted Chambers. "But I could save twenty just as well."

"Just as well," Jerome agreed, "in heaven."

"Now, look here," asserted the mentor, figuring on the edge of a newspaper. "I pay, counting in my dinners down town, ten dollars a week for my board and room. Two hundred and fifty a year for clothes — and that's outside, clear outside — is five dollars a week more. There you have everything — board, rent, clothes, for just half my salary."

"Well?"

"Well, if one can live on half a salary, two

can live on the whole of it. Jerome," he broke
out suddenly, " let's get married."

" To each other ? "

Chambers passed the flippancy in high silence.

" What do you say ? "

" No, thank you," replied Jerome, tranquilly,
wondering whether the rush of blood in his
veins was really like a river.

" Oh, the d——l! " exclaimed Chambers.
" I forgot the laundry."

" Don't wash," suggested Jerome.

" But we could work it in on the clothes al-
lowance."

" We ? "

" You and I," explained Chambers, red to
the roots of his hair.

" Oh, yes, of course, you and I."   Jerome
was observant of nothing. " You could wear
clothes, and I could wash."

" Good night," said Chambers.   But the
next evening, about one o'clock, he came rushing in again, surprising Jerome in his favourite
occupation of nights — thinking, thinking,
thinking. " Put it there, old man," the boy
cried, holding out his hand, " I'm engaged."

He was too pleased with himself and the world to sit still; he roamed about the tiny room, knocking over this and that and apologizing without interruption in his stream of talk.

"I thought I was immune," he said; "but I've got it bad, Jerome. The first time I saw her, you know, I thought that she was a plucky little woman; but afterward, when I saw how much there was in her, well, I thought, Bill Chambers, if you're a man at all, you'll freeze to this girl, if you can get her. Last night I just had to say something about it to you; but those figures cooled me down so I didn't think I'd ever get back to the point of asking her. I went over there to-night, and, by George! I hadn't been there ten minutes when — well, put it there, Jerome."

Jerome did so once more. "But who, Will?"

Chambers laughed. "Don't you know yet? I thought I'd said her name a dozen times, but maybe it was just the sound of it in my own ears. Her name's Mary — Mary Wilcox, and you've seen her."

"I?"

" Don't you remember the night we went over on West Adams about six weeks ago? "

" Oh! the little girl who cried! "

" Yes," said Chambers, proudly. " The little girl who cried, and wouldn't leave another girl who was dead, because the other never liked to be left alone! I hate to think of that night except for that one thing. How plucky she was!" His eyes kindled.

" Are you thinking of getting married soon? "

" I don't know. Give me time to breathe, Jerry! why, I've only been engaged three hours — or maybe five. I've got to be submitted to the old folks, yet. They live down my way — about fifty miles south of our town, that is, in Boonville. By George, Jerry, what do you think? that little girl of mine is up here by herself, earning twelve dollars a week as stenographer in a lawyer's office, because her father hasn't very much, and she wants her two brothers to go through college. She's afraid of everything in the world; she's afraid to death of this big old town here, trampling all around her; and here she stays by herself, so that her father can help her brothers.

o

Pluck — don't talk to me about pluck, Jerry, or I shall lose my head and cry."

" Is she," Jerome asked slowly, " in that same place? "

" Not she," replied Chambers, briefly. " I helped her move the second time I called."

The Northrops, mother and daughter, returned to the city in October. They had been, as usual, making a round of Eastern watering places, and Mrs. Northrop professed herself perfectly exhausted by her summer. " Next year," she insisted, " we really must stay at Lake Forest, Elsie; the town is growing really delightful now that the golf-club has been established there. Don't you think so, Mr. Kent? "

" I should like Lake Forest very much, mamma," answered Elsie, quietly. She had heard, at the end of every summer for some years, this threat of Lake Forest for the ensuing hot weather. But in the spring her mother's fancy had always lightly turned again to thoughts of the East. Jerome fancied that Elsie Northrop had grown quieter, if possible, than before; more staid, more marble-like. When he took his leave, and she followed him into the hall, he was astonished.

" Will you come to see me to-morrow evening, Mr. Kent? " she asked, almost hurriedly. " I have a special reason.   I want to see you alone."

" I cannot come to-morrow, I am afraid," he answered.   " There is a meeting of assemblymen I must attend.   The next evening? "

" If you will, please," she answered.

What special reason, he wondered, could this still, calm young woman have for seeing him?   He recalled her father's phrase, on the day at Lake Forest when Jerome had retaken his vows, and so, unwittingly, destroyed his own life.   " A special reason for seeing you."

He called at nine o'clock, and she came down, as he had expected, alone.   When she gave him her hand, it was not cool and firm, as before; it was cold, and shook a little.   There was a spot of colour in her face.   Her voice was as steady as ever, but plainly she was under the stress of some emotion.

" You must not think it strange, Mr. Kent, that I should ask you to come to see me," she said, after a minute, " nor that what I am going to ask you is strange — though it may seem so. My father has told me a great deal about you, Mr. Kent, and about your life, and what you are trying to do. I hope you don't think me impertinent in telling you this, or in knowing more of you than you have told me?" She stopped.

"No, no," he answered quickly. "It is very kind of you to take any interest at all."

She did not seem to heed his answer. "You must know that my father is much interested in you, and is very fond of you? He said once, when you had just come, that he hoped we should be like brother and sister. If we have not — well, you know, Mr. Kent, that you have not seemed to care for us very much." She phrased the fact calmly, as though there were in it, or in her phrasing of it, nothing surprising or unusual.

"If I have seemed," he began. But Elsie interrupted.

"You have been all that you should be," she said. "Don't think that I am trying to reproach you. No; I am going to ask you a very strange question, and I wished that you should know just why I asked it of you. Mr. Kent, what is the matter with papa?"

He stared.

"Have you noticed nothing?" she asked. "You have been here with him constantly, and the change had been so gradual, perhaps — But when I came back I saw at once. He is thinner; he is more restless; he hardly ever talks to me any more."

"He is overworking," said Jerome. "He is very busy with the paper, you know."

"Have you noticed nothing else?" she asked. Her eyes, clear, honest, mournful, were fixed upon his. He thought rapidly. Was the shade of wonderment that had crept over him, now and then — at Lake Forest, and in Northrop's private office, for example — when the old man's voice rose and his eyes gleamed, and his thin white fingers worked nervously — was that worth speaking of; so worth that he should run the risk of adding to this young girl's anxiety? He wondered what she had seen. Her deep eyes still demanded honesty.

"Yes," he answered slowly. "I have noticed something."

She drew a long breath that was almost a sob: as if she had hoped against the fact. "What?" she asked. He told her, as quietly as he could. He made it nothing, nothing at all — a tightening of the lips, a restless movement of the fingers, an occasional quick look.

"Often?"

"No.   Only, I   think, when — "   He paused.

"When   he   spoke — perhaps — of — Mr. Wheeler?"

"Yes,"   Jerome   said   gently,   "then   I think."

"Oh," she half whispered, "it is true!" She looked at her fingers locked together in her lap, for some minutes.

"It is nothing," he urged finally. "I am certain that it is nothing. Your father is a man who has very strong public spirit, and he has been working in the public interest against Christopher Wheeler for a long time. Now he sees an opportunity to accomplish something, and he is working harder than ever; that is absolutely all. I hope, for his sake, that he will accomplish what he wants and defeat the gas bill; he will be bitterly disappointed if he does not. But, at any rate, when the strain is over, he will be in that point as he is in all his other life now, willing to rest when he has worked too hard."

"You must be right," she answered. "You will understand, won't you, Mr. Kent, if I tell you that I am very tired?"

"Yes," he replied. "You said, a little while ago, that your father had hoped we might be like brother and sister. Will you let me — sometimes — help you, if I can, in little things, as your brother might? You will make me very proud, if you will."

He fancied that she swayed a little when she rose to take his hand. "I shall be glad of a brother. I have always wanted one, you know. You won't speak of this to my mother, please? She is not strong; she would worry, when I know, as you say, there is nothing to worry over. You will come to see me? Good night — Jerome."

"Good night, Elsie," he answered.

He came again a few nights afterward to dinner.

"You must blame Elsie," Mrs. Northrop told him, "that you are dining *en famille*. I wanted to have some young folks in — George Hayward, and Alice Montgomery, and Ruth Adams, and people like that, of your own age. But Elsie insisted that you would prefer not.

I told her I was sure I didn't know how she could tell what you preferred, and certainly it would only be natural that you should want young people, but I had to give in, as I always do. Elsie is very strong, Mr. Kent, when she makes up her mind — oh, very strong. I always say that I hope her husband will be a demon, or she will do as she pleases even after she is married."

"In the fairy story," answered Jerome, " Beauty was too much even for the Beast."

" Was she? " asked Mrs. Northrop, politely, if a little vaguely.

Jerome, watching Northrop with eyes sharpened in anxiety, was shocked at the change in him; shocked at himself for not observing it sooner; shocked at his wife for not seeing anything amiss. Northrop ate little, and talked even less. He fell into fits of abstraction, from which his wife would rouse him by some question which the old man, with a start and a little smile, would answer, when it was repeated. The blue veins on his eyelids were traced as clearly as a map on white paper, and his hands were as delicate as an invalid's. Only his clothes were as careful and punctilious as ever.

Jerome, too, wore evening dress to-night. In less than half a year the young man from Scannell County, Indiana, had taken on the external appearance of the cosmopolite.

When dinner was almost over, Mrs. Northrop suddenly bethought herself of a topic full of interest to her, and to them all.

" James," she requested the footman, " bring me to-night's *Herald,* please. Elsie," she went on, " don't you remember that the last time Mr. Kent was dining here, just before we went away, when Judge Hetheridge and Margaret Walton were with us, you spoke of Mr. Wheeler's daughter — what is her name? Ethel — coming out this fall? She came out this afternoon; there is a great picture of her in the *Herald.* It is very pretty. I have never seen her, but they say she is really quite wonderful looking."

" Have you ever come out, Mr. Kent? " asked Elsie, suddenly. " I don't see why men shouldn't as well as women, do you? "

But Jerome was too startled to play up to Elsie's lead. *She* was in the city, then! she had come out that day, as she had said she some day would! her picture was in the *Herald!*

His thoughts were interrupted by the words of his host. Elsie looked up.

" Poor girl, poor girl! What has she come out to but dishonour and disgrace?" Northrop's whole face was illuminated with sorrow. Then his eyes shone again. " But the children must suffer for the sins of their fathers!"

James brought the paper. " There!" pointed Mrs. Northrop, triumphantly, handing it to Jerome. " *Isn't* she pretty?"

It was the same photograph that he had at home, but greatly enlarged. The eyes were happy in spite of themselves, the firm mouth softened into curves. She justified the garishness of print, redeemed the vulgarity of this public exhibition. Were your eyes like that as you held up your roses, Ethel? Did you smile or sigh? Did any one see the traces of tears you might have shed the night before? As you stood there in your father's great house, hearing the compliments they showered on you, did you ever think of the days when you had wandered through the June? Jerome looked at the picture. Suddenly he heard a quick breath taken. He glanced up. Elsie Northrop's eyes met his, full of wonderment. The red flush came into his face, into his forehead even, and then slipped back. But he saw that she had seen.

" No picture of her father? " said Northrop, smoothly. " Oh, well — we shall give them reason to publish it one of these days, perhaps."

" Have you seen nothing in all this summer, new to tell us about, Mr. Kent? " asked Elsie, determinedly.

" Oh, yes," he answered. He began to recite the story of a woman's club meeting he had reported, where the lady president resigned in anger, and then when they accepted her resignation accused them of being unparliamentary — " to say nothing of impolite," she added. And so the dinner ended. Afterward, Elsie sang again, songs her father preferred — ballads of Ireland and Scotland, full of strange minor chords that sobbed like children. Mrs. Northrop played; the old man sat with shut eyes, dreaming; Jerome, too, listened in a dream; she was interpreting his wonderings.

When she finished, Northrop excused himself and went away to his room, and soon afterward Mrs. Northrop followed. She liked to talk, but not to this young fellow with sombre eyes, who seemed hardly conscious that she was talking at all.

"I saw you looking at the picture," Elsie said abruptly when they were alone.

"Yes."

"When did you meet her, Jerome?"

"In June," he answered simply.

"Do you know her well?"

"Yes; I knew her well."

"I am your sister," Elsie said in a low voice.

"I love her, Elsie," he added.

"Ah — poor, poor boy!"

He told her the story, finding it a great relief to tell some one.

"And you have never seen her since?"

"No — never once."

"Do you think she cared for you?"

"She told me she did not. But — almost always I believe she did, a little."

Elsie wondered what Jerome's plans were, how he hoped to free himself from the tangle. But she only said quietly, —

"I hope more than ever that I can be a good sister to you, Jerome."

"Thank you," he replied.

"What did you think — to-night — of papa?" she asked in a moment.

"I think, as before," Jerome said slowly, "that he is overworked, that is all."

"Did you see any change in him when my mother mentioned Miss Wheeler's name?"

"Yes," he admitted, hesitating.

"I must ask mamma to be careful," she added in an even voice. "I should have done so before, but I don't like to frighten her."

"It was good of you," said Jerome, "not to let her have people here to meet me. I am very stupid company these days."

"Oh," she returned, "I was thinking of papa, not of you. I am afraid I used you as a scapegoat."

Jerome went to another dinner early in November, at which there were present only three — Chambers, and the little girl to whom he was engaged. Chambers took him to call, first. She was afraid of him, as the young reporter predicted she would be.

"Don't mind if her hand shakes when she gives it to you," Chambers counselled. "She'd be afraid of me if I stopped talking

long enough to give her a chance, and the Lord
knows what she'll think about you, you dreary
old hippopotamus.   Try to cheer up a little;
don't look at her as if she was your best
friend's funeral."

"I shall laugh uninterruptedly," Jerome
promised.

"Do," said Chambers.

But the two got on as well as even the anxious journalist desired.   "I hope you don't
mind," Jerome told her, "if I claim a share in
Will.   You see I knew him first."

"He speaks of you very often," she answered timidly.

"I hope he speaks well of me," Jerome said;
"for what I am is mostly due to him.   I don't
believe that on one day this summer he has
failed to give me some good advice."

"Piffle," cried the delighted reporter.   "The
only advice I can give you is what Solomon
gave to the Queen of Sheba.   'Go thou and do
likewise!'"

"I don't believe," Jerome answered firmly,
"that it was Solomon who said that, or that he
said it to the Queen of Sheba.   Was it, Miss
Wilcox?"

" Miss ? " demanded Chambers.

" If you say he is right," Jerome insisted, " I shall call you Miss Wilcox, for then I shall know you are willing to sacrifice me and the truth to him. But if you prove me correct, I shall call you Mary."

" It was not Solomon," she replied, blushing.

" There, Will ! " he   nodded   soberly. " Thank you, Mary."   When they went away she held him a moment at the door. " Will, go on a minute, please," she begged. " I want to speak to — Mr. Jerome — just a minute."

" Ah, *would* you ? " answered Chambers. " The first night I bring him over — and to do it so openly, too ! " He kissed her and stepped into the hall.

" That night, Mr. Jerome," she went on hurriedly, when they were alone, " when I saw Will — and you. I wanted to tell you — if you were afraid for Will — that she and I — were not very good friends. We were rooming next each other, and I knew her before — And then, afterward — when she told me — I could hardly have gone away — and left her alone — could I ? " Her voice shook.

" Being you," he returned, in a low voice, " I suppose you couldn't."

" Well," she trembled on, " I wanted you to know — because you were there — in case you were afraid for Will."

He looked at her small shrinking figure, and the blue eyes that looked straight into his while the voice wavered.

" No," he said, " no, Mary, I am not afraid for Will. I think that if you stay by him nobody need to be afraid for him."

" What was it ? " asked Chambers, curiously, when they were in the street.

" She was trying to make me fall in love with her," answered Jerome, calmly. " And, Will, she nearly did."

" Piffle ! " returned the delighted Chambers once more.

CHAPTER X

NORTHROP was hard to hold as time went on. The facsimiles on which he based so much expectation were ready to be struck off at any time, and Hanlon found need for all his tact to keep the old man from putting them out prematurely. Northrop had almost succeeded in convincing himself that, once published, this list would do all the work he had been planning so long — defeat the gas bill, indict Wheeler, cleanse the whole political atmosphere of the state; and he grew more and more anxious to bring off the coup at once.

But Hanlon held him in check, with the assistance of Jerome's influence.

The legislature convened on the 8th of December, but Hanlon and Kent arrived in Springfield on the 6th. On the way down, Hanlon explained the situation as he understood it.

"You know, Kent, I'm here to get the news. Personally I am opposed to this bill of Wheeler's, but I didn't come down to fight that or any other bill, I came to find out what is going on. You, I take it, are here, as a matter of fact, to lobby against Union Gas. Well, the first thing, you need to be acquainted with the country members; know all you can." He drew from his pocket a list of the membership of the legislature. " Here I have marked all the names as Wheeler had them marked on the list you got. It is a great thing to know exactly your enemy's strength and calculations. Looking at this, you see, we can tell exactly what his plans are; he is all in the dark about ours. Well, here I find, in the lower House, 125 names marked O. K. and 112 marked N. G. That leaves 33 out of 270 who have figures attached. That means 125 men will vote for Wheeler, and 112 are no good to him.

" Of course, you needn't trouble yourself over those marked N. G. If Wheeler had come and *told* you he had given up trying to induce those men to vote for his bill, or if he had allowed you to find out that he had stopped working on them, that would be different; then you'd want to look after those fellows night and day. But this piece of evidence you got is absolutely straight, you see ; he doesn't

know you've got it — does he?" he asked abruptly. Jerome shook his head. No inquiries,
so far as he knew, had ever been made for the
red-leather pocket-book.

" That, then, is all right. Now about these
men marked O. K.; you can't do much there,
either, perhaps; still, when you have a chance
with one, find out all you can. Something may
have come up, you never can tell; the remun-
eration may have all gone, by now, or if he's
honest, he may even have changed his views.
But the real set you want to get after is the lot
with figures behind their names — the thirty-
three.

" There are two or three things to consider.
First, some of those thirty-three may be what
Union Gas would call O. K. by now. In other
words, they may have been *seen* already. On
the other hand, mighty few of them would be
put down, even now, as N. G. on the old man's
list. The agitation hasn't been quite hot
enough yet for the honest ones, and the others
are simply hungry, and will bite at the biggest
bone, no matter who throws it out. In the next
place, you've been on this work long enough
to know that these figures don't mean money.

If all one had to do in putting through anything crooked, was to go to a man with a thou-
sand-dollar bill and say, ' Here's for your vote,
take it or leave it,' as if it was a fifty-cent piece
and a tramp outside a polling place — if bribery and corruption, as they say, was that easy,
the big corporations would own the country in
two weeks, from the President down. But it
can't be worked in just that way. Now and
then money passes, real coin, but not often.

  " Suppose your name was Jenkins, we'll say,
and you'd been elected to the legislature from
down in Pohasset County, fifty miles from a
town over ten thousand. You're a lawyer with
a good growing family, and mighty little to
put into their mouths; you've done well by the
party, made some speeches about the eagle and
the flag, and you're not strong enough to be
dangerous; you can be trusted to vote for the
party men every time. So they elect you to the
legislature. Well, you are glad, of course ;
you come up to Springfield, take a room on a
back street and eat at a hash house, draw your
five per diem and send four and a half home to
the wife. Meanwhile, you wander round with
your toothpick in your mouth, and you see

other fellows, whose vote counts one, just as yours does, opening champagne in the Fountain House. Do you ever get a little discontented, Jenkins, and write home to the family, maybe, that things don't seem equally divided in this democratic country? Yes, I think you do.

"By and by comes a measure that isn't by any means a party affair. The corporations want something, and that is always the signal for a scramble of patriots on both sides. They find out — probably they've known it all along — that Jenkins of Pohasset County is in the legislature with a vote counting one. They look up Jenkins of Pohasset County — country lawyer, large family, excellent character, member of the church, never gets drunk — man of unblemished reputation. Then they send a man around to you."

"And he fixes you," finished Jerome.

"And he does nothing of the sort. He's a fellow legislator; it's his business to find out whether you have the proper idea of the legislature, which is, that it's a close corporation, like the Masons, where, if one brother is found doing something a little off colour, the others go round the corner for a few minutes; not like a church, for instance, where you are pledged to bawl and yell the second you see anybody stepping to one side. In other words, it's bad form to split on a member of the fraternity. This legislator comes around, then, and puts you right on that point, if you aren't right already. If Wheeler is part of the corporation maybe Arkell comes, maybe Laramie, maybe Benson; maybe somebody else.

" *Then* they get at you. You're to be convinced of the worth of the bill first, if possible. But sometimes it's a lovely bare-faced steal, so that plan can't be tried. However, take this gas bill, for instance. You, Jenkins, come as I said from a town of five thousand; what do your constituents care for a bill which affects only Chicago ? So long as it's not a party measure, they won't call you down; they'll give you a free hand, and if later you have your house painted and send the younger boys away to school for a year, they won't mind; the drinks are on Chicago, anyway. You know they won't mind; you are one of them.

" Now a man comes to see you who knows you, who has made it his business to know you. You get to talking over things, and he asks you

how the law business is in Pohasset County.
You tell him it's pretty poor scratching. 'Get
a good many railroad cases though, I suppose,'
he says. No, you tell him, most of those go to
Robinson, further up the line. 'Well,' he
says, 'that's too bad. I know Mr. Blenkinsopp,
who's a director; know him well. If you
won't consider it intruding in your affairs, I'll
just speak to Blenkinsopp about you.' You
don't consider it any intrusion; *you* know who
Blenkinsopp is, and you know too, that if this
man speaks to him it means a nice little five
hundred a year, perhaps, on your income.

" ' Oh, by the way,' he says later, ' have you
made up your mind about the gas bill ? That's
a good bill, I believe; it has its faults, so they
all have, but I shall vote for it, and I hope you
can see your way clear to voting for it also.'
Only he doesn't call it the gas bill; he calls it
House Bill No. 7742.

" Well, what happens? either you are a fool
and don't understand the influence, but simply
give him your vote out of gratitude, when the
time comes, for his help with Blenkinsopp; or
you aren't a fool, do understand, and have
to make up your mind. You don't care a rip

about Chicago, you know; the newspapers of Chicago abuse the bill, but what of it? they are always howling about something. Here's five hundred a year coming your way. What do you do, Mr. Jenkins of Pohasset County?"

"I see," replied Jerome.

"Well, then, it's for you now,— not as Jenkins, but as yourself — to get to know Jenkins, and all the rest of them. Most of them are honest enough; and when their principles are aroused, they'll do what is right. You've got to educate them. The *Eagle* and the other papers will do the foundation-work of pointing out the demerits of the bill, and letting nobody rest in ignorance that influence is being used. You will have to do the rest. When we get to Springfield, you'll find many of the country members already there, looking about. You must get acquainted at once; get them all to like you. You can't fight money with any weapon but friendship."

"It's a big contract," suggested Kent.

"Fighting money always is," sententiously replied the political editor of the *Eagle*.

The weather was bleak and drizzling. Springfield was in the midst of the untidiness that always precedes a holiday. Two days later, when the legislature convened, the wreaths would be up and the floors swept; now everything was a litter of preparation. As they rode up to the Fountain House, the water on the car-rails splashed into muddy streets. The lobby entrance of the hotel was paved with sloppy oil-cloth.

"It won't do you much good to look at the register," explained Hanlon. "The men *you* want don't room here; they live back on the side streets. This is the O. K. house. But ten to one some of your meat will be lounging around here. We'll go out and have a look." It was as he said; in five minutes Jerome had been introduced to three — Hartley, Meek, and Wilcox — all marked, as he remembered, 500 or 1000 in Wheeler's estimate.

"Mr. Kent a journalist, like yourself, Mr. Hanlon?" asked Hartley, a pompous old man with a gray beard.

"Yes, he's a newspaper man," answered Hanlon, "on the *Eagle.*"

"Excuse me," diffidently remarked Wilcox, "but are you Mr. Jerome Kent? Do you know anybody by the name of Chambers?"

"Very well," replied Jerome, heartily.

"He is — the fact is — well, I guess my eldest girl's going to marry him," went on Wilcox. He was a small man, of hesitant address, like his daughter. A sandy beard covered the weakness of his chin. His eyes were china-blue — in a woman they would have been called appealing. He was of that type of men who seem to deprecate their own existence, and whose coat of arms should bear a homeless dog, *couchant*.

"Let me shake hands again," said Jerome. "I haven't known your daughter long, Mr. Wilcox, but I respect her more than I do most people; and Will Chambers is one of my best friends."

"So Mary wrote," the legislator answered, rubbing his hands together nervously. "I guess — I guess he's a very good fellow. Hey?"

"Suppose we celebrate this meeting of acquaintances," Hanlon suggested. He had largely laid aside the dry, cynical air that characterized him in Chicago, and adapted a pleasant species of *bonhomie*.

"Mr. Hartley, what's yours? Mr. Meek? Mr. Wilcox?"

"I — I will take a — a lemonade if you please," replied Wilcox.

"Br'r," shivered Hanlon. "You'll have to sit on a radiator to drink it, Mr. Wilcox. What do you say to a hot milk shake — if you don't like stick?"

"Thank you, I should prefer that," answered Wilcox.

"I should like to call, if you don't mind, Mr. Wilcox," said Jerome, in a low voice as they stood at the bar. "I feel as if I had found a friend down here already, since we both have such an interest in Will — and your daughter. You are not stopping at the Fountain House?"

"No, oh, no," answered Wilcox, "I am not — not stopping at any hotel at present. I am at a private boarding-house on Fourth Street, 122. I should take it very kind of you to call, very kind."

"I shall do so to-morrow," Jerome returned. "Shall we drink to — them?"

"It is — it is a pleasure, Mr. Kent, to do so."

Jerome made the acquaintance, as Hanlon advised, of many a legislator in the next few

days, before the legislature convened, and afterward. Generally, they fell into types, with
slight personal differences—the pompous type,
represented by Hartley, formal of speech, careful to preserve a congressional dignity, but
commonly ready to take a drink when asked;
the genial, hail-fellow-well-met men, who spoke
in loud, cheerful voices, called every new acquaintance by his name, without prefix, and
saluted him with a slap on the shoulder; the
men from the inland cities, Peoria and Rock
Island and Quincy, less devoted to the frock-
coat, some of them smart young fellows in the
early thirties, who showed a distinct crease
down the front of the trouser-leg, and turned
up those garments at the bottom even on dry
days; many other types, of course, but these
the most prominent. And he met men of the
craftier sort, two or three, men like villains on
the 19th Street stage, men who were known
openly as " out for the stuff." They, too, if
they were not marked " O. K." on Wheeler's
list, were put far down on the scale as easy
prey when the time came. The genial men,
who talked freely, as birds sing, never revealing a secret in all the long day; and the quiet

men who scarcely talked at all, great men for committees : these were the sort he valued highly, whose vote was estimated in the thousands.

He met Arkell and Laramie again — old acquaintances in Chicago — who asked him humorously if the *Eagle* were still screaming, and whether he knew that, after all, House Bill 7742 would not come up this session.   House Bill 7742 was Wheeler's bill.   No, Jerome said, he didn't know that; he must wire the *Eagle* at once, as he believed the news was a scoop. " And certainly it's very good of you, Mr. Arkell, to put us on — under the circumstances." Arkell's fat sides shook with laughter.   " I see you wag your tail too fast to let an old man like me drop salt on it," he said admiringly. " What the h——l is young Kent at? " he queried of his colleague a few minutes later. " The *Eagle* never sent two men down here before.   This young fellow knows half the country members already; I never see him without somebody we need in tow.   Is he lobbying? "

" Probably," consented Laramie.

" They say old Northrop's going cracked," added Arkell, contemptuously.   " I didn't be-

lieve it before, but I do now. Why don't he
send a baby down here?"

The work was not so unpleasant as Jerome
had feared. He gave up all idea of trying to
trace any ill-doing back to Wheeler, and contented himself with forming acquaintances that
might be useful in the future. It was true, as
Arkell said, that in two weeks he knew half the
country members. They interested him; from
the country himself, he understood their ways
of looking at the world, could appreciate with
exactitude the stretch of their horizons. And
he was learning much from the unconscious
Wilcox, who after a few days accepted him on
trust and told him many things. Wilcox's case
was the embodiment of that which Hanlon
had sketched in the train. Wilcox might have
sat for the portrait of the supposititious Jenkins. His views on the gas bill were vague,
indefinite. It would be a good thing, he supposed, to have the matter settled definitely;
would keep business from unsteadiness. But
he really hadn't looked into the matter much.
He told Jerome about his family. He was evidently fondest of Mary, but proud of his two
sons, who were in college at Jacksonville.

"One of them a senior and one a soph-o-more," their father said with pride. "You are a college student, of course?" No, Jerome was not.

"Neither am I," sighed Wilcox, with evident relief. "Not so many colleges in my day," he added. Then there were the three younger children, left at home with his wife — two more boys and a little girl — "a girl at each end," as he said.

So the session went on for a few weeks, and Jerome was working almost hard enough to forget all he wished to forget — almost, but not quite. Still, in the night before he went to sleep, he could not help fancying a face he knew, with clear, shining eyes and a firm mouth, looking at him from the darkness. He had left the little photograph at home. He had not the heart to bring it while he was fighting with all his power against her father. Meanwhile the gas bill, in spite of Arkell's humorous remarks, had been promptly introduced and had gone to a second reading. When at the Christmas recess Hanlon and Jerome rode home together, the political editor confided to his assistant that the time seemed to him ripe for publication of the facsimile.

" It's bound to be soon," he added; " the old man is getting away from me; it's a hard matter to be telling your employer every day what he's to do. Anyway, it's up to us, I think. The campaign here in Chicago, between the *Eagle* and the *Eye,* has been pushed along pretty lively. The public is excited now; everybody's watching the bill and wondering how it will come out. I think I shall tell the old man to let the rocket go on the 4th of January, the day before the legislature reconvenes. The 4th is on Sunday, and we have a big Sunday circulation in the country districts. Jove, Kent, do you know, I actually begin to get a little excited over this thing. It'll be the biggest piece of Chicago journalism in years; the old man will have to have a special clerk to file away the libel suits. I believe, if I were in his place, I'd give it up even now; it's too risky; I'd lose my nerve." He yawned, looking out at the backward-flying banks of snow on either side of the track. " But there's no giving up in Henry Northrop. Kent, I'd like to ask you a question, if you don't mind. I don't need to tell you I'll keep it quiet; you know me. But how did you get hold of that list ? "

Jerome glanced up. " I thought Northrop told you," he replied.

" That day in the office ? "

" Yes."

" So he did," confessed Hanlon. " This lad's no fool," he thought, " and he's quite right; the fewer in the know, the better. But I'd like to know just how he managed it. Good God, what a newspaperman he'll make when he knows the ropes ! "

Northrop, when Hanlon rendered his decision, was overjoyed. " You think the 4th of January is best ? " he asked. " I should like to make it a Christmas gift to the city — the downfall of Christopher Wheeler. But I agree." Even in the three weeks since he had left Northrop, the old man had changed for the worse, Jerome could see. The suppressed excitement about the facsimile was wearing him out rapidly. Jerome was glad that it would be over soon. His own work was not done until Wheeler's measure was defeated; was not done even then, perhaps, if Northrop held him to his promise. For Jerome's mind, as any one can have guessed by now, was made up on one point. He would stick to his prom-

Q

ise to his father. He had been wavering in the balance; he had decided to do what he conceived to be his duty, and immediately he was made to suffer in a way of which he had never dreamed. Then he had set his teeth like a bull-dog. His pride would pull him through now. When he could look at his dead father's handwriting, and say, "Father, I have kept my word!" then — well, what then? Jerome did not know. Perhaps life would be over; perhaps he could make life begin again.

He saw Elsie and had a long talk. She mentioned with some shyness that she had met Ethel Wheeler. "Of course, father does not know. We spoke only a word or two. She is very pretty, Jerome. But she looked very tired. She isn't popular, in spite of her beauty, they say; she hurts people's feelings too much."

Elsie did not say much about her father. "I think he is about the same," she admitted, "only tired. I spoke to mamma about his needing rest, and she was very good; we have few people in, now, and I am sure it is better for him. I sing to him every evening, and he goes to sleep."

Chambers and his fiancée were not in the
city; they had gone down to Boonville to
spend the holiday.   "My, but you made a
hit with papa-in-law-to-be," wrote Chambers.
"It's Mr. Kent, Mr. Kent, till I grow jealous.
I told Mary I intended to have the wedding before she saw you again, so as to avoid any pós-
sible hitch in the proceedings."

Jerome was invited to spend Christmas Eve
with the Northrops.   On the afternoon of the
24th he wandered down to the office at his old
accustomed hour.   He wanted something to
do.   McKinney easily supplied the want.   "I
won't give you a school entertainment to-day,"
he grinned amiably.   "How should you like to
beard a lion in his den, a Douglas in his hall?
See here; here's a note from Chris Wheeler,
saying the *Eagle* misquoted him yesterday, as
usual, and wanting us to send up a man to rec-
tify it.   Will you go?"

The plan caught Jerome's attention.   "Yes,"
he said after a moment.   He repented his
words as soon as he was out of the office.   Suppose he should meet Her!   But it was too late
to turn back.

Wheeler received him after a long wait, in

his private room. The great man sat at his desk, dwarfing it. His huge red head, only slightly tinged with gray, still flared like a torch above shoulders little less massive than the deformities of the Farnese Hercules. His big hands against his immaculate cuffs were stubby, coarse, and powerful as hammers. His clothes were expensive and showy; his eyes, deep-set, wore red rims; his nose was bulbous and more veined than of old. Otherwise, as he had faced the father years before, the son saw him now.

"Young man from the *Eagle?*" he growled.

"Yes, sir."

"D——d scandalous sheet!" exploded the old man. "I don't care what it says about me, but when it takes to quoting my words, I want 'em right — right, do you hear? Tell your boss he'll have a suit for libel on his hands when I get around to it. Meanwhile, — take out your pencil. Now write this down as I say it, word for word." He dictated. "There!" he said. "Now get along and see how much you'll twist that, going from here down town."

On the side of his head, running up into his

hair, showed a freshly healed broad scar.
Jerome stared at it curiously, while Wheeler
bent over his desk. The old man looked up and
caught his eye.

"Well, what now?" He put up his hand.
"Wonder what made that, hey?" There was
no indication in Wheeler's tone that he had
taken offence. "That was where they tried to
hold me up, awhile ago. That would have finished most men, eh? I'm tough, young man;
I'm tough. You tell your boss I'm tough, will
you? Tell him he can't get at me till he can
hit harder than most of 'em. I don't mind his
lies. Take a drink, young man; I've nothing
against you; only you're working for a d——d
poor stick, that Northrop. Why don't you get
a *man* for boss — eh?"

"The man who gave you that scar hit
pretty hard, Mr. Wheeler," said Jerome. "I
fancy he hit harder than most men."

"Nearly laid me out, not quite."

"Pretty nearly," acquiesced Jerome, incau-
tiously. He was thinking of the old man's appearance that night, and his cry — "Blood all
over me!"

"What do you know about it?"

"It looks like a nasty blow — that's all."
Wheeler reflected.

"How came it that the *Eagle* knew about
the hold-up, and nobody else?" he demanded
suddenly.

"It's an enterprising paper," answered Jerome, lightly.

"D——d enterprising," growled the old
man. "What's your name, young man?" he
asked suddenly.

"You can call me Smith." Jerome had
no intention of arousing old memories in
Wheeler. In a way he was wise. The thought
of John Kent was the sorest spot — one may
say the only sore spot — in Wheeler's mind.
For nothing else in his long career was he
ashamed; he rather took credit for his astute-
ness, for the unsportsmanlike abuse he had got
from the men he had beaten. But this man,
Kent, smaller than himself, who assaulted him
only with his tongue, Wheeler had struck; and
Kent had died. He did not feel guilty, but he
felt that he had lowered his own ideals to strike
a smaller man. To bear abuse patiently, to win
to his own ends, and then to take revenge, —
that was Wheeler's code. Not all of us live

up to ours as sincerely; not all of us when ours is broken feel such remorse as he. No, the name of Kent would have called back to Wheeler the face of a dead man. But the subterfuge woke other memories.

" By G——d!" he cried, " I believe you're the man that I've been looking for!"

Too late Jerome realized his mistake. This might jeopardize the publication of the facsimile! He gathered up his papers and rose.

" Good day, Mr. Wheeler."

" No!" thundered Wheeler. " We'll have a few more words first, before you go. *What's come of my pocket-book, young man?*" His deep-set eyes glowed, and his whole big body swelled with the demand. " You know the man who made *that* hit harder than most of 'em, don't you? A little more and you'd have done for me, eh? but you just missed. *Now,* I'll try what I can do with you!" He whirled up the big office chair on which he had been sitting, as if it were a feather. Murder was in his eyes as plain as print. With one motion Jerome jerked open the office door, with another pulled it to behind him. There was a crash; the broken chair smashed through the panels. There was the sound of a fall, and then — silence; no pursuit. Jerome stood panting in the corridor a moment, then went hurriedly down the broad stairs. At the foot, in the gloom of the great hall, he met Ethel coming up. It was the first time he had seen her since the day by the lake.

"Is there anything —— ? " she said quickly. "I thought I heard a noise." Then she saw him plainly. "Oh!" she cried, and covered her face with her hands.

"There is an accident — or — something — I think," he answered briefly. It seemed to him that he was in a dream. "I should send up a servant, if I were you."

"Papa?" she cried again. "I will go up." She brushed past him. He waited irresolutely; he could scarcely leave her alone to face — what? He did not know. As he stood there he found himself thinking, mechanically, "How beautiful she is! How beautiful she is!" But only for a moment. Suddenly he heard her scream.

He turned and ran back up the stairs. The door of the office was open; she sat within, her father's head in her lap.

" Is he dead? "

" No," she said with an extraordinary calmness, " he has a fit, I think. I wish you would
telephone for Dr. Evans — there is the telephone in the corner. His number is Main
9641. Ring for the servants, please." Jerome
rang; then, while among the fragments of the
broken door and chair Christopher Wheeler
breathed stertorously through blue lips, his
head in his daughter's lap, telephoned for help.

When the servants came, frightened, intoler-
ably curious, he went away; it seemed to him
the only thing he could do. He walked down
to the office with Wheeler's dictation in his
pocket. His mind was in a terrible whirl, but
one fact stood out clearly — when she saw
him, before she had time to think even, he
had seen in lips and eyes that she was glad. In
spite of everything, then, he was happy.

CHAPTER XI

JEROME wondered that night at Northrop's how much of the day he should tell Elsie. That the events of the afternoon were finished, without more ado, he did not for a moment believe — unless Wheeler died in his fit. He knew that even then he would be called upon to explain his presence in the house. But he decided to say nothing until he was asked. He had reported at the office that Wheeler was taken suddenly ill while he was there. McKinney raged at him for not staying to cover the affair, and then sent two other men up in hot haste. Jerome knew that McKinney would give no information to the reporters of other papers, who might find out from the servants that a man from the *Eagle* had been present at the time. They would not, probably, even seek to find out who the *Eagle* man had been; they would only curse at his good luck. He whispered to Elsie, therefore, only that Wheeler had

234

had an accident that afternoon, and that he might be dying. She thought it best not to tell her father. The late afternoon papers contained the news in flaring headlines, with very little under them. Access to the house had been denied to all. Even the dailies of the following morning had accounts meagre in fact, though padded with speculations. They all published the doctor's bulletin; Wheeler was suffering from a stroke of apoplexy, brought on by overexertion. He was unconscious, but in no immediate danger of death. Some of the Wheeler servants resigned and left. The angry fits of their master, when he broke furniture and threatened personal violence, generally had this effect. Others stayed on; the wages were good. The holidays wore on, and the sensation failed to be sustained. The Saturday following the New Year Jerome and Hanlon left again for Springfield.

On the 4th, Sunday, was published, as planned, the facsimile of the list of the legislature, with notes in Wheeler's writing. That the writing was Wheeler's was explained; a facsimile letter of Wheeler's showing the same turns of N's and G's, and many of the same

figures, was published below.   That was all.
An editorial comment, however, double-leaded,
signed by Northrop himself, drove the matter
home.   It was calm, clear, cogent; as Jerome
read it, he felt his fears for Northrop dissipate.

The effect of the publication is too fresh in
the minds of every one to need description here.
Of the rage of some men, and the satisfaction
of others — depending largely on the notes set
opposite their names; of the disbelief of many,
the dozens of suits for libel that were quickly
filed, as Hanlon had predicted; of the sale of
that edition of the *Eagle,* of which in expectation of the demand, three hundred and fifty
thousand copies had been prepared, all of which
were exhausted by ten o'clock in the forenoon;
of the request of a New York daily, which
offered by telegraph twenty-five thousand dollars for the original document from which the
facsimile was made, to be doubled if the document proved not to be a forgery — nobody has
forgotten these things, at least no one in Illinois.   Hanlon was right, as usual; the publication was the biggest newspaper sensation in
years.   Wheeler's suit for libel, claiming half a
million dollars, was recorded on Monday morn-

ing. It was preceded, eighteen hours, by the
arrest in Springfield of Jerome Kent, charged
with robbery, assault and battery, and attempted murder. Wheeler had recovered from
his stroke of apoplexy three days before, but he
had delayed his hand. In the first place he
knew who the young man from the *Eagle* was,
now; Jerome Kent, son of the John Kent of
old acquaintance; in the second place, he had
understood the fact that he had no evidence
against him. When he recognized the list for
the one he had lost on that night, he wasted no
time; here was evidence enough; the warrant
of arrest was made out and telegraphed to
Springfield. It was not until the next day,
when Wheeler came to file his suit for libel, that
he realized that there was still no evidence —
such as he could use — against young Kent. If
he adduced the list as evidence in the criminal
case, what was the effect on the suit for libel?
He hesitated long, even then. There was a
moment when he thought he would acknowledge openly — yes, the list was his, the handwriting was his. He would pin the robbery on
this devil, and send him to his deserts, at any
cost. Then he gave that up. The list he could

not, dared not—even he, Christopher Wheeler, dared not — acknowledge.   The libel suits might be turned against him, then; at any hint of his that the list was true, his bill was lost immediately, his influence gone forever.   And he could not afford to lose that bill!   He cursed the mines which had swallowed his money, as he had cursed them often before.   But he would press the case against young Kent, at any rate; he would leave no stone unturned to convict him; he would swear to the truth himself, and his word would have weight.   Bear in mind that in Christopher Wheeler's mind, that this young man, his old enemy's son, had struck him and robbed him, there was no shadow of a doubt.

Hanlon, Northrop, and Jerome talked the matter over before Jerome consulted any lawyer.   Northrop had bailed Jerome out within three hours.   He was useless in the conference; his fingers clutched and writhed, his eyes shot fire, he proposed schemes impracticable as suicide!

"You see," Hanlon said, "you are in no danger, for the only evidence against you Wheeler cannot possibly use.   If he dared to say 'That list the *Eagle* published was in my pocket-book the night they robbed me,' things would begin to look black. He could easily prove who brought the story into the office, you know; the deduction would be for the jury, and they would make it unless you had a mighty good lawyer. But you are safe, because that's just what he daren't say. If he did, he would step into his own coffin."

"See here, Hanlon," returned Jerome, calmly, "I may be wrong, but it sounds to me as though you thought I was guilty, and wanted to squirm out on a technicality. Do you think I slugged that old man and robbed him?"

"Yes, I do," answered Hanlon, directly.

"You're wrong," replied Jerome. Hanlon looked at him keenly, and then reached out his hand. "Glad to hear it," he said briefly. "I've been admiring your sand, but all the same I'm glad, to hear it. Well, now," he continued, "we can discuss this more in harmony. The question is, now, not how to bring a man off free, but how to prevent an innocent one from any injury. As I say, I can't see where you can be touched. He'll swear he recognized you just before you hit him — I'm saying what he will say, understand. But a clever lawyer will rip that recognition in ten thousand pieces. If he can recognize you as the robber now, why couldn't he when you took him home on the same night? If you were the robber, would you be likely to publish an account of the affair? Where is there any evidence of robbery at all?"

" I burned the pocket-book," cried Northrop. " I burned it myself here in this grate. Oh, yes; I took care of that."

" Well — then that's all right," answered Hanlon, in a mild voice. " And you're as safe as government bonds, Kent. Are you going to see a lawyer now? Come along."

" Get the best," counselled the old man, keenly, cunningly. " Get Woods. Of course, you will have no expenses anywhere."

Hanlon and Jerome went out. " Come into my office," demanded Hanlon, when they had descended to the sixth floor.

" Do you know where your danger lies, Kent?" he asked when they were alone. " It's in *the old man*. He thinks you've done this, just as I did, but he's wild to get you off, of

course. That would be all right. But I believe he's cracked." Hanlon sat back to see
how Kent took his statement.

" Why? "

" Why? Look at him," answered the political editor, quietly. "Listen to him! He
shouted out there that he'd burned the pocket-
book as if no one was within a thousand miles.
Yes, Kent, I believe he's crazy; and the best
thing his people can do, if he's got any, is to
put him in a sanitarium right away." He
touched his hair with a small comb before a
mirror on the wall. He was as impassive as if
he had been discussing dishonesty in the presi-
dential chair — if one can imagine such a
thing. He returned to Springfield that night,
leaving Jerome to follow in a day.

Should he tell Elsie, Jerome wondered, what
this man thought? The quick resolution came
— he must. He had seen very little of her, of
course, lately. Now he was to confront her
with more trouble. But she deserved honesty,
if ever a girl deserved it. She took the news
as quietly as ever, when he called that night.

" I have been wondering that people did not
see it," she said. " Poor papa! "

R

Jerome took her hand. "And you?"

"I have done all my crying," she answered. "I must look out for mamma and my father now."

"Had you not better talk the matter over with some one — Judge Hetheridge, for instance?" he suggested. But she shook her head.

"Not yet," she answered. "What could he do, that I cannot? And — I don't want to be the first to point out — anything wrong — with papa."

"But you spoke of it to me," he urged.

"Yes, Jerome," she said.

"Thank you, Elsie," he answered. Could he intrude on her what Hanlon had suggested — that in Northrop lay danger for him? He went away even ashamed that he had remembered it. The rest of the evening he gave to Chambers, who was wild with excitement. That Jerome stood in any danger of conviction Chambers could not believe; and so the mere fact of his being arrested and out on bail surrounded him, in the young reporter's eyes, with a kind of romantic interest. "Dick Turpin" he christened him at once, and wove a string

of adventures about him — the modern robber, of improved parentage and with improved
methods.

" Oh, Jerry! " he cried with delight.   " I
have got something for my people — in the stories — to do and say now ! Thanks, old man,
thanks ! Who cares for the dramatic-critic
business now ? Old Hengle can hang on till
his fingers cramp, if he wants to; it's going to
William Chambers now, the Chicago short-
story writer, vice Richard Harding Davis resigned — and you shall have half the profits,
Richard the highwayman ! "

Early the next morning Jerome was off once
more to Springfield.

CHAPTER XII

AFTER the indictment the trial was pushed rapidly on; neither side desired any delay. Meanwhile the affairs of the gas bill, which had been in extreme peril, were taking a slight turn for the better. The prompt institution of Wheeler's libel suit, although expected, had, nevertheless, some effect. The publication of the facsimile list had been, in short, so bold a stroke that it had been almost too bold; its boldness, taken in conjunction with a rumour or two which began to creep about, that Northrop of the *Eagle* was not the man he had been once, made many doubt the genuineness of the document. The men who were marked " O. K." had many of them been known as open supporters of the bill; the men marked " N. G." were known as strong opposers. Why should not the rest be guesses; libellous, of course, but what was an action for libel against a big city paper, anxious for a sensa-

tion? Such was the reasoning in the country
districts; and the men of the list began to recover their equanimity, and even those marked
with figures to wonder, some of them, whether
they might not after all vote for the gas bill
when it came up. It was delayed, to give just
this feeling a chance to grow.

"The trial comes off before Hetheridge,"
Jerome's lawyer said. "That is not unfavour-
able to us; he is no friend of Wheeler's. Besides, he is altogether the best man. Some of
the rest of them may know more law, but he
knows more human nature, and I shall base
a good many of my objections on human nature."

"I know him."

"Personally?"

Jerome nodded.

"Want a change of venue?" was the sus-
picious lawyer's next question.

"No, indeed," answered Jerome. But he
remembered — how far back it seemed! — the
first day he had come to Chicago, seven or
eight months before, and had met the Judge at
his club. The Judge had warned him humorously to keep away in business hours. Now he

was going in business hours, nevertheless. He wondered if the Judge would remember.

The Judge remembered. It was most unprofessional of him to do so, but he remembered. He remembered also one night at the Northrops', when the old man had begun — " Kent has a feud with Wheeler, you see," and then had checked himself. Now Hetheridge wished young Kent would take a change of venue. But he was not unprofessional enough to suggest that.

The rooms of the criminal court are never without their crowd. Faces among it become almost as well known to the bailiffs as the face of the judge. Men, and women even, find in the courtroom their stage and their stadium. And yet one trial is to the ordinary spectator very like another — the judge and jury above, the ring of lawyers who advance toward them, and converse in tones so low the ears often strain vainly to catch the words; the long dull succession of witnesses, endeavouring with more or less success to tell or conceal the truth; the reporters lounging or scribbling in their choice seats, envied by all; the crowd, shifting, curious, silent, the great blue German or Irish policemen, swollen with majesty and beer, and the accused in his special chair. To the judge, to the lawyers, to the looker-on, one trial is very like another. It is only the accused who catches the note of individuality, finding *his* trial, out of myriads, still unstaled by commonplace. There is, however, a certain element of difference which to some extent regulates the size of the crowd. If the case has been widely advertised by the newspapers; if the principal is a man of reputation, good or very bad; and especially if there is over the matter the veil of a mystery which must be torn across, then the people come — the people who love to see the twistings of a fly on a pin and of a man on trial for his character or his life. Then the professional attendants, as one might call them, the habitués, are swallowed up, lost to view in the tide of new faces. In a little while the attraction ceases; the tide recedes; and they reappear once more day after day. The case of the State *versus* Jerome Kent seemed to involve no mystery; not more than fifty people in Chicago, perhaps, knew Jerome by sight; but, because it was well understood that this case grew out of the long and deadly struggle be-

tween the *Eagle* newspaper and the Union
Gas Bill, between Henry Northrop and Chris
Wheeler, the crowd came, filling the courtroom.

Northrop insisted upon being present at
every session. That he was rapidly going to
pieces under the strain of his fight was an open
secret now. In the month between Jerome's
arrest and his trial, the old man aged ten years.
He was a shadow of himself. His physician
insisted upon his retirement to a rest-cure, to
the South, anywhere to get away from the
strain that was killing him. But Northrop
paid no attention. "I have my work to do,"
he said angrily, if he answered at all, when
they remonstrated with him. He went two
and three times a day to consult with Woods,
until that busy lawyer warned his doorkeeper
that he was out to Northrop. He would stare
at Jerome, in the two days before the trial,
when Kent came up from Springfield, for fifteen minutes without speaking, and then, smiling, with the glint of his old smile, whisper,
with a glance around to see that he was not
overheard, "Never mind, Jerome; it is safe.
I burnt it myself." With a pang Jerome realized that, as Hanlon said, the old man believed

him guilty, and was only conscious of getting him free at any cost. Now and then Northrop fell into fits of black abstraction; grew despondent; once he advised Jerome to forfeit his bail, offering to supply him with all the money he needed to go anywhere. Jerome gently declined. From these fits Northrop quickly recovered, and resumed his attitude of cunning confidence.

The trial began on the 4th of February. On the day before, sitting in his little room on Huron Street, which he had kept even while he was in Springfield, Jerome spent a long hour thinking over his past year. To-morrow he was to be examined for the assault and robbery of the father of the girl he loved, the girl who loved him. Surely he had tangled his affairs badly in this first essay of life! Was it all his own fault? He had been bound by this old promise, and it had pulled him here. He believed that, proved guilty or innocent, his life was wrecked. He might still be successful, but he could not be happy. He was a young man whose ideas of life were gathered largely from books. He knew that he was deeply and finally in love with a girl now forever separated from

him; and he believed that he could not love
again. If only he might have had counsel, at
the moment, from some person of hard, prac-
tical common sense, who could have told him
that only in literature is one love all; that in
life we love, and love, and love again! And yet,
who knows? Perhaps the ideals of literature
are now and then as true as the truths of life.

He recalled the day that he had met Her, and
their unconventional and close acquaintance;
the day she had for the first time failed to
come; and the day she had gone away forever.
He thought of the night he had brought her
father home — for which he now stood on trial
— and how the next day he had found out his
own miserable unhappiness. He knew that
after all he was not as innocent as he had led
Hanlon to believe. He had not assaulted, but
he had robbed. Robbed was the word. He had
stolen the property of Wheeler, and though he
had stolen it for no advantage or profit of his
own, the crime was nothing less. If he were to
put himself on the stand, and tell the story exactly as it happened, with no further accusation
or charge from Wheeler, he would still be found
guilty on the law, and sent to prison. Was a

man, then, so innocent if he dared not tell the
truth of the matter in which he was concerned?
Wheeler judged him wrongly; but Wheeler's
judgment was not wholly in the wrong.
Thinking of all this, Jerome felt that he had
forfeited his right, the right Ethel Wheeler had
unconsciously given him, to see her again, tell
her he loved her, and demand again to know
if she loved him in return; and so he determined to destroy her picture. He went to
the drawer where he had placed it months before, but it was not there. He searched the
little room thoroughly — an easy task — and
could find no trace of it. He summoned Mrs.
Kenealy. Had she seen a small photograph, of
such and such a sort, at any time, in his bureau
drawer? She repudiated the idea with a cold
asperity. She was not in the habit of looking
in her lodgers' bureau drawers! He came to
the conclusion that some one among the curious
maids, attracted by the picture as she turned
over his goods, had slipped it away. When he
realized that it was gone, he knew at once that
it would not have been possible for him to destroy it. His heart ached as though some one
had torn a piece away.

He stood his trial on the following day. The room was crowded; but as the hours wore on, and nothing happened but the reiterated questions of one side or the other, as juror after juror was drawn, followed by the Judge's " Excused," or the rare peremptory challenge, the morning slipped away. The afternoon session was like the morning. The whole day was consumed in securing a jury, but at last they were all there, measurably intelligent, measurably honest — the jury of his peers, ready to decide whether Jerome Kent should wear a spotted name or not through life. To them, too, this trial was individual and interesting. One of them was a young fellow of twenty-three. As he sat in his place with the rest, a conscious smile rested continually on his lips; and Jerome knew that the boy felt the eyes of the whole courtroom to be upon him, and enjoyed them. After that, Jerome himself was less nervous, more at ease. He realized that the focus of attention was a little divided.

He remained that night in the jail. They gave him whatever he asked for — paper, and pen, and books. He wrote and read all night, quite unable to sleep. The prison horror crept upon his sensitive nerves. What should he do, he wondered, if they found him guilty? On the following morning, when the actual trial began, he appeared haggard in his chair.

The prosecuting attorney outlined his case. They would prove the prisoner had struck the blow; they would prove that he had possession of the pocket-book. Such were the salient points. He was confident and debonair. Woods was contemptuous. He outlined the truth. Kent had assisted the old man home, and then reported the matter to his paper, and had gone home to bed. Neither lawyer spoke a word of what was in every man's mind — the list and the facsimile. Both sides desired to keep it out of the case. The state's attorney called Christopher Wheeler, and the manipulator of Union Gas got upon the stand. In him, as in Northrop, the month had wrought changes. His eyes were more sunken, or his face puffier; his voice was hoarse and disagreeable, not the lion's roar it had been once. The scar still lay upon his forehead, running into his hair; and from time to time, as he gave his evidence, he touched it with his hand.

He identified the prisoner positively as the

man who had struck him. Had he recognized
him a few minutes after the assault, when the
prisoner returned? Objection by Woods to
the form of the question; sustained. Very
well, said the state's attorney. He had recognized the prisoner a few minutes later, as the
man who had struck him? Yes, he had; he
was, however, dazed and bleeding, and could
not think what to do. What had the prisoner
said when he took him (Wheeler) home? He
wanted to go into the house. Why? To finish
his job, the witness supposed. Question and
answer stricken out; but not before they had
had their carefully calculated effect upon the
jury — and the spectators. The admission by
the prosecution, that Kent had helped the old
man home, had been thought a weak spot in
their case. Why should a highwayman do a
thing so kindly? Here was a plausible reason
deftly slipped in. The boldness of the fellow!
The crowd was actually tickled, and began to
look at Jerome with admiration.

Wheeler went on with his testimony. He
had never been able to find his man, until a
month and a half ago, on December 24, the
prisoner himself came to the house to inter-

view him — for the *Eagle*. He had recognized him at once. The excitement had
brought on a fit of apoplexy. Cross-examined,
he admitted the probability of his assault on
Jerome that day, though he denied knowledge
of it. The fit must have been on him then,
for he knew nothing, from the moment of
recognition, to the next day. Otherwise he
stuck to his story; growled; would not be
shaken. When he stepped down, he had made
as strong a case as could be expected, but
Woods was satisfied and calm. " Nothing in
it," he said in Jerome's ear.

Jerome himself could see that the old man
had confined himself — necessarily — to asser-
tions. They called then two or three minor
witnesses, to prove that Jerome had brought
the account of the assault into the office.
Woods did not cross-examine. He would have
admitted all they swore to, without hesitation.
Jerome made no denial that he had been on the
scene a few moments later, and helped Wheeler
home.

In the noon recess Woods was confident to
the point of gayety. " As the case stands," he
said, " and it seems to be about finished, there

isn't a point against you. What Wheeler said goes for nothing. Nothing links you to the blow, nor to the robbery. He says yes, you say no; your word is as good as his. When the prosecution finishes, I shall move that the case be taken from the jury."

Jerome assented with a nod. The sickish feeling of abhorrence still lay on him like a weight. What if they found him guilty? As he sat in his chair through the morning, he told himself over and over that Wheeler wanted mere revenge; that justice demanded no penalty from him. He would have hesitated to pay it, at all events, for since his single night in jail freedom seemed a matter fiercely to be desired. He agreed with the lawyer, now, in anticipating a quick and happy verdict. If they could have used the facsimile against him, their task would have been easy. But they could not use it, and other evidence against him there was none. He should have been supremely confident. But only certainties, finished contests, can give entire confidence or despair to the contestant himself.

After luncheon he resumed his place. The room was as full, when he was brought in, as it

had been when he left it. He wondered whether
all those people had sat there motionless while
he waited outside. He looked out over the
crowd, enveloped in the odour, though not the
haze, of tobacco. There were hundreds of
faces turned to his, which he had never seen,
eyes which found him only a character in a
yarn, an actor in a drama for their amusement.
But among them he saw some he knew — Northrop, sitting by Hanlon, quivering, haggard,
and old; Chambers, his jollity gone, tense now
with anxiety and hope; men from the *Eagle*
in the reporters' seats; Victor sketching
calmly; and Hetheridge, his red face gloomed
with judicial solemnity. The reporters said
that something was wrong with old man Hetheridge; not a joke had he sprung in the trial,
but sat cold and stern as ever Jeffries was.

Now the prosecuting attorney recalled Christopher Wheeler. The old man had insisted on
it. During the noon recess he had been chafed;
he thought the case was going against him;
rather than see it so, he would dig up his dead
past, and show cause, between these two, of
hatred. So the state's attorney put the questions Wheeler had told him to put, and brought

s

out the story of the old feud. Wheeler, sitting
with deep-set red-rimmed eyes, his strong old
face never changing, to ruin the son gave evidence how he had killed the father. Perhaps
when he was in the current of the recital he was
sorry he had once begun; but one does not
know. At least, he told it steadily, unwaver-
ingly, sternly. But Northrop grew more
nervous every instant, as the truth was established that something like a vengeance toward
Wheeler had lain upon Jerome's back. Hetheridge, too, sitting moodily, hearing the end
of the story Northrop had once mysteriously
begun to tell him at the dinner; sitting in the
midst of the trial, as he stared at the young man
in jeopardy of his good name, Hetheridge
forgot again his rigid, superhuman, professional ethics, and wished that young Kent had
taken a change of venue. One must remember occasionally that a judge is only a man.
Wheeler stepped down without cross-examina-
tion. "Not worth while," whispered Woods.
"This doesn't touch the facts."

The prosecuting attorney called William
Edeson, a name wholly unknown to Jerome.
The prisoner was full of a fierce anger now.

His own case faded from his thoughts;
there was his father's to be considered.
Wheeler, who had killed his father, now
boasted of the crime; told it openly in court;
used it against his father's son! He allowed
Woods to let the old man go without cross-ex-
amination. They might have blackened
Wheeler's reputation, but to what end? Was
it not black enough already? And if they bore
upon the fact that Wheeler had in effect mur-
dered the elder Kent, they just so far aided
Wheeler by establishing Jerome's motive.
What the boy wanted now was to get free
quickly; and then — and then — Jerome
allowed the thought to cross his mind that *then*
there might be a trial in which Wheeler would
have something to complain of. But the man
William Edeson was undergoing examina-
tion.

His name? His profession? Detective.
His connection with the case he told. He had
searched the prisoner's room, and had found
— did he recognize this photograph? Yes;
he had found it there. He detailed the circumstances.

"I desire to introduce in evidence this

photograph of the daughter of Mr. Wheeler," cried the state's attorney. " As I shall prove, it was in Mr. Wheeler's pocket-book on the night he was assaulted and the pocket-book taken from him. We have shown that it was discovered later in the prisoner's room. Have I your Honour's permission? "

" I told you to burn it, I told you to burn it!" The voice, shrill, agonized, and shivering, rang through the courtroom. " I told you to burn it, I told you to burn it! " Northrop was on his feet, his eyes blazing, his whole body trembling; Hanlon attempted to pull him down; the audience sprang up in amazement. The Judge rapped fiercely with his gavel; the big policemen, seizing men one in each hand, crushed them down. " Order, order! " But the voice rose a third time in a scream, " I told you to burn it, I told you to burn it! " Two bailiffs, crowding in, attempted to take him away, but the old man struggled fiercely. At length they led him out. The state's attorney stretched out his arm with dramatic gesture.

" Who can hide truth for long? " he cried.

" I object! " Woods, too, sprang up. " Such incidents cannot be presented to the jury except when properly introduced as evidence."

"Objection sustained," answered Hetheridge. "Gentlemen of the jury, you will disregard, in your deliberations, the words uttered by spectators."

"But I would call your attention," proclaimed the state's attorney, recovering his suavity the instant Hetheridge ended, "to the photograph just introduced." And the routine went on.

But the prisoner was turned to stone. It is easy to say that when he missed the picture he should have foreseen this end; had he confided in Woods, the lawyer would have told him that at once. But the suspicion had never come to Jerome. That the revengeful old man could drag even his daughter, even Her, into the mud of such a case, he would have found unbelievable, if to him it had not been unthinkable at all. Now he desired only to get away alone with his sorrow. It was intolerable to sit there before the crowded room. From fierce anger to numbing grief he had been hurried in a moment of time, and his nerves were shocked and blunted so that even

Northrop's cry failed to reach his heart, and his old friend's pitiful breaking-down was like a play before dead eyes. He felt dimly but surely that his case was lost; nothing he could do, no objections Woods could enter, no ruling of the Judge, would blot from the minds of those twelve jurymen the wild sincerity of Northrop's cry. When the state had shown that the photograph was in Wheeler's pocket-book the night he was robbed, the case for the prosecution was ended. The defence had no witnesses to introduce. Woods urged that the case be taken from the jury. No evidence, he asserted, had been brought out to connect his client with the assault; for Wheeler's recognition of him, dazed and bleeding as the victim admitted himself to have been, was patently a farce. The photograph had come into his client's possession through circumstances which only the chivalry of his client — and here his client, stolid in his chair, quivered perceptibly — the chivalry of his client, in marked contrast to the curious brutality of the young woman's own father, prevented him from detailing. And so he proceeded. " The prosecution has admitted," he finished, chang-

ing his tone, "that my client, Mr. Kent, helped
Mr. Wheeler home — truly a genial highwayman, full of courtesy, and to the manner
born! It has more than admitted, even gone
to the trouble of proving, that my client had
published an account of the robbery — truly a
bold highwayman, whose deeds of evil, contrary to the Scriptures, love light rather than
darkness! I ask, then, that your Honour take
the case from the jury and dismiss it."

"Denied," said Hetheridge, in the usual me-
chanical judge's voice. He gave the jury the
usual instructions briefly. "The jury will retire and consider upon their verdict."

When the jury had gone out, there was a
buzz in the courtroom, quickly hushed by the
bailiffs. Few went away; there seemed a general feeling that the verdict would be quickly
returned. Jerome sat with his eyes on the
floor. He did not see Chambers, his face
drawn, searching with his eyes the door of the
jury room; the reporters writing like mad;
the empty seat of the Judge; nor the curious
crowd.

"Hold tight," said Woods, "for I think
they have beaten us, my boy." He had his

own sorrow; he had, he feared, lost a case
that he might easily have won if his client had
trusted him. But there was something in
Kent's attitude that overcame, for the moment, his impatience with pity. The Judge
returned, the jury filed in. The old, old for-
mula began.

"Gentlemen, have you considered your verdict?"

"We have. We find the prisoner at the bar
guilty as charged in the indictment."

"Is this the verdict of each of you individually?"

"Yes, sir."

"Mr. Clerk, poll the jury." It was done.
Jerome still sat with his eyes on the floor.
Even the words of the foreman could scarcely
touch him now. To-morrow, perhaps.

"Will you have sentence pronounced now?"
The crowd hung on the answer. Would the
prisoner disappoint them here in the last scene
of their play?

"Now, if you please."

"Stand up." Jerome stood up mechanically, mechanically heard and comprehended
the words of the Judge. "One year in the

penitentiary, to serve at hard labour until dis-
charged." The courtroom was cleared, and
they took him back to his cell in the jail.

Few short trials have afforded the city more
entertainment than these two days in which
Jerome Kent was found guilty of assault and
robbery. The dramatic introduction of the
photograph would alone have made material
for the papers, since Miss Wheeler was now
almost as well known as her notorious
father. But the collapse of Northrop startled
the whole town. The *Eagle* only, on the following day, confined itself to simple facts,
much to the disgust of the many who bought
it to secure inside information. Overwork,
under the strain of the contest over the gas bill,
the *Eagle* said, had brought about temporary
mental aberration in Mr. Northrop. Mr. Northrop was now under the care of physicians in
his house at Bass Avenue, and, it was hoped,
would speedily recover. Editorially, the *Eagle*
commented on the state of politics in America,
when through general public apathy one man
could be forced on and on in the effort to
overcome, almost single-handed, the leagued
forces of evil, until human nature could no

longer endure. There would be no cessation in the contest against the Union Gas Bill. The *Eagle* took occasion to announce once more the genuineness of the document in its possession, of which a facsimile had been published.

Meanwhile, in the house on Bass Avenue, an old man wrung his hands and shouted constantly, "He should have burnt it, he should have burnt it!" while his daughter repeated as constantly, over and over again, "It is burnt now, papa; it is all right now." Elsie was right in saying she had done all her crying. She was so self-possessed, now when her long fears were really culminated in truth, that finally the doctor even grudgingly admitted she might possibly stay alone with her father, provided the male nurse remained close outside. Northrop showed no tendency to struggle, at length, but was contented to sit still in an armchair, looking with vague eyes out upon the grounds, through a locked window. It was Elsie who guessed that he would sleep if she sang, when for thirty-six hours his eyes remained obstinately open. Later, it was Elsie whose slow voice began to have its effect on the disturbed brain, so that only

now and then he would demand doubtfully,
" Did he burn it? " always to meet the steady,
even answer, " Yes, papa, it is burnt now."
So she coaxed him slowly back to poise again.

" I cannot leave papa, even to come and see
you, my brother," she wrote Jerome two days
after the trial. " I cannot even write you
what I should like, for I have not the words.
But you know, I think, out of the depths of
your sorrow the depths of my sympathy and
belief. It will come right, Jerome, it will
come right. If I were not sure of that, how
could I be sure there was a God at all? "

Not a word, in all the long letter, told of her
own devotion, or hinted at despair. It was a
letter that comforted a little even Jerome. A
week afterward he was taken to the penitentiary, and began his service.

CHAPTER XIII

'A BRISK and alert young man of twenty-five
or six stepped off the train at Joliet one morning in the following May. He glanced with
an air of proprietorship at the buildings adja-
cent to the station, looked at his watch, and
jumped into a cab. " To the penitentiary,"
he said curtly, and lay back to consider the
world while the carriage bumped over the May
streets which characterize the ordinary Illinois
towns. He had been married only a month,
and he found it difficult to be unhappy, in spite
of the fact that he was about to see his closest
friend, and that his friend was a convict of the
state penitentiary. It was " visiting day " at
Joliet.

And yet, when he actually had Jerome before
his eyes Chambers found his spirits sinking
readily enough. The hideous misshapen uniform, the cropped hair over the broad forehead,
the clumsy shoes, blotted out the personality of

his friend, and presented in his stead, not
Jerome Kent, but convict 963. It was only
when he looked at the eyes that Chambers
could shake off the depression lying upon
him.

"How are you, old man?" he asked awkwardly enough.

"Very well, Will," Jerome answered, in the
slow voice the inmate of a penal institution so
quickly picks up. "How good it is of you
to come out here and see me!"

"Nonsense!" Chambers shook himself, as
if he were throwing off something that hung
about him. "Now, Jerry," he went on,
"we've only got half an hour, and I think
the best way is for you to fire off questions on
what you want to know, and I'll answer 'em.
First, though; I'm married."

"Already?"

Chambers nodded. "Hengle left at last, a
month and a half ago; and they put me in the
dramatic critic business, and jumped me to
forty a week. So we put it through." He
laughed. "I like it, Jerry."

"I'm so glad, old man."

"Well — fire away."

"I'm afraid I can't do that, Will," answered Kent, slowly. "Won't you just tell me what's happened — if you'll be good enough?"

Chambers eyed him curiously. Jerome was not as depressed as he had expected, and yet he was more quiet. Was this self-humiliation, this careful politeness, healthy, Chambers wondered? Aloud he went on, —

"What do you know, Jerry?"

"Not a thing, Will. I haven't read a paper or heard a word from outside since I — came down."

Chambers fairly jumped. "What!" he cried, "don't you know about Wheeler, and about Union Gas?"

"No," answered Jerome.

"The bill was lost," said Chambers. "Shall I tell you about it?"

"I'd rather hear it than anything else," Jerome replied simply.

Chambers, standing close to the grating, shifting his position from time to time, talked hurriedly and in a low tone.

"After — you know," he said, "when Northrop went loco, the gas bill began to pick up a bit. You see, pretty nearly all your work down at Springfield — well, Jerry, when that damnable jury put you in here, the people that you know down in Springfield talked. I even had a row with Mary's father, by letter, over it. He seemed to think you'd been string-ing them all, him included. I told him you were all right, but of course I hadn't any evi-dence except your word, and — well, he was a specimen of the lot of 'em, and I'm thankful Mary takes more after her mother in a good many things. Then Northrop's words in the court hurt his reputation; and as people had got to thinking a good deal that Union Gas wasn't so much a question of right against wrong, as of Henry Northrop against Chris Wheeler, they began to favour the Wheeler side a little more. In the end, everybody saw when the bill came up it was going to be nip and tuck, pull husband, pull bear. Wheeler was spending big money, everybody knew, and be-sides, he was buying more Union Gas stock on margins, and making thousands every day; for lots of people shared his confidence in the bill's passing, and Union Gas went on rising slowly right along. You never saw a man

so confident as Wheeler was. Your trial,
you see, and Northrop going off the handle,
made him think nothing could stand up
against him any more. They say he was
painting the town red every night, too, but I
don't know anything about that. They sent
me up to his house one night, and George, but
he was big! He wanted me to drink some of
his whiskey, but my! I couldn't have swallowed any of the old liar's best, if it had been
seventy-seven years old. 'From the *Eagle,*
eh?' he said. 'To hell with the *Eagle!* You'll
find Chris Wheeler's a little too big for you,
young man!' When I was coming out I met
his daughter. She didn't see me by a hundred
yards, but I saw her, and she's worth looking
at. Jerry, she's a queen, though the good
Lord knows where she gets it from."

"Go on," interrupted Jerome.

"Oh, yes — well, for once even Jimmy
Hanlon didn't know how a bill was coming
out. Of course, I was interested, and Mary
through me, and what did we hear all of a
sudden but from Mary's father that he was
going to vote for the gas bill! When Mary
told me I swore. She wanted to know why,

and I explained for the dozenth time about you, and Northrop, and Wheeler. She seemed all cut up for two or three days. Finally, nothing would do but she must go down to Springfield and see her father. She did; and she went alone. I couldn't have got off, but she wouldn't have let me go with her, anyway. She wouldn't tell me what she went for, even; but since we were married she did, and said I might tell you. Jerry, do you remember the girl who committed suicide over on the West side, the night I met Mary,— the Jewish woman? And you remember why she killed herself? Jerry, *Wheeler was the man,* and Mary knew it all along; and that's what she told her father.

" Well, you know him. The gas bill people had offered him a big thing — a place for himself, and one for Frank, who gets out of college in a month. He didn't put it that way, of course, but that's what it amounted to; and he is mighty hard up, and hates to see his family growing up without knowing anything. They think they'll have to take Tom out of college next year — but they won't, unless the *Eagle* reduces my salary. Well — when Mary told

T

the old man, she cried, of course, and he cried too; but he wouldn't say he'd vote against the bill. And in three days, just before the end of the session, it came up in the House. Everybody knew the fight would come there; the Senate was a cinch, and the governor was bought and paid for. They called the roll, and it came on closer and closer, and when Wilcox's name was called, he could decide it. Well, I'm not proud of papa-in-law, particularly, but he knew if under the circumstances he voted for the bill his fortune was made. Mary was down there, in the galleries, and the old man knew that too. Instead of voting, he began to explain. He rambled ahead, Hanlon told me, and they all thought, of course, he was going to vote for the bill and pick up the wad. God knows what he meant to do; but my poor little girl, who had been sitting in a front seat for five hours, couldn't stand it any longer; and she began to cry. The old man looked up and saw her. 'I vote *No!*' he broke off, and sat down. They say for a minute you couldn't hear anything but Mary crying, all by herself; and then — hell broke loose. They telegraphed the news up to Wheeler over his private wire. His secretary had gone out for something just before the news came; when he came back, in a quarter of an hour, the old man was dead on the floor."

"Wheeler dead!" Jerome cried. Chambers nodded.

"Apoplexy again. When they went to work on his affairs, they found out he'd left about two million dollars in special bequests to a lot of colleges, and the residue to his family — wife and daughter. When the bill was defeated, Union Gas slumped thirty-five points in ten minutes. What do you think Wheeler's estate will amount to, when they settle for his margins and straighten out a lot of fussing in mines, and such stuff — speculations he's been handling the last two or three years? They say in the city that he won't have fifty thousand in the world, and if those colleges claim *pro rata* the family will go on the streets."

"Where are they now?" asked Jerome.

"In their house, waiting for it to be sold. They say it's a fearful shock to the old woman. But if she has any sense, she won't fret. The gentleman that's gone is better dead, and her daughter is sure to marry money and take care of the two of them. My, Jerry, but she's a queen!"

"The Northrops?" asked Jerome, hastily.

"They say the old man is getting better. His daughter takes care of him, and he's doing well. They say he doesn't know anything about the gas bill, or Wheeler's death, or anything like that; they daren't tell him, and he doesn't ask. It's funny the two of you who were so much concerned in it, should be the last ones to know how the whole thing came out!" commented Chambers. "But, say, old man, I haven't heard a word about you yet. Can you — stand it here?"

"Oh, yes," Kent said cheerfully, "I stand it very well. They are as good to — us — as you could expect. I could have seen the papers if I'd wanted, but I've fallen out of the habit. They let me write letters, too, one a week, and receive them. But I haven't written any yet."

"I've got one here for you," returned Chambers, "from Miss Northrop. How shall I get it to you?"

"Give it to the warden, please. It must be read first, you know."

"Well — I can tell them all you're feeling pretty well, eh? Everybody, all the old crowd wants to hear how you are, and they all send their love, or would have, if they knew I was coming down. I'm sorry I couldn't come before, Jerry, old man, but we can't get off just when we please, you know, — and then getting married and all!" he finished.

"Yes," replied Jerome, "it was mighty good of you to come at all, Will! Yes, you can tell them, if they ask, that I am feeling pretty well."

"Time's up, sir," admonished the warden.

"Good-by, Jerry," said Chambers, "au revoir, old man, au revoir."

"Au revoir, Will." And "visiting day" for Jerome Kent was over.

But that night he had his letter in his cell.

"Are things coming out right, Jerome? I am sorry that I cannot see you, but I think of you all the time. I have a great deal of time, now; papa likes to have me with him; he doesn't want to talk, but he seems to grow a little restless if I read. So I have a great deal of time to think. Papa is growing very much better, I am sure. He is not so thin, now. He talks a little, sometimes, usually about the things he used to see —the flowers. He hardly ever asks me if I have burned the photograph, and he does not look about him in that frightened way.

"Dear Jerome, I was not sure whether to write that about the photograph; and I am not sure whether to tell you this; I have seen Ethel Wheeler since her father died. Her poor mother is almost distracted, they say, but Miss Wheeler seemed to be wonderfully strong. And Jerome, if you ask me how I saw her, I must tell you. I wrote to her and asked her if I might. Was I so wrong? I do not think so. I told her all the story, just as I knew it from you — how you had found the pocket-book, and how you had kept the picture. I cannot tell you what she said, or what she did, dear brother. But she knows, now, and she believes.

"Are you working — writing? or are you only thinking and growing wise? I do not know what they let you do. But I am sure you are not desponding. We have both had our little troubles lately, haven't we? Perhaps they are big enough to last all our lives long.

But I do not think God sent them to crush out our lives, dear Jerome; and I still believe in a God."

He lay a long time that night on his narrow iron bed, thinking over the letter and Chambers's news. He could appreciate the loyalty which made the one girl keep the other's secret. And yet he wished that Elsie had told him more of what She had said. She knew, now, all of his life; why he had been opposed to her father, and why he had been, once, dishonourable. Was he right in opposing her father? Was he wrong in his dishonour? He had been bitterly punished for both. Why had he been allowed to live his quiet, even life so long, and then suddenly thrust into the whirl and turmoil of things, to spin about and drift, at last, broken, down the stream? He, or fate, had so brought it about that all his determination and efforts counted for nothing. He had fought, and had won nothing. After all his toil, Wheeler's downfall was brought about by Wheeler's own wickedness and folly, and suddenly accomplished by the weeping of a girl. Had he, Jerome Kent, nothing to show for his life but lost honour and a stained name? Once, when he was a child, he had gone out picking wild raspberries; and, having fallen, he had come home, at the end of a long, hot day, bruised, with torn clothes, and not even one berry for his labour. Yet he had meant well on that day, as on this. And was he, as a man, to expect the comfort and petting that he had received then, for meaning well?

His thoughts turned again. What was She doing, and what would She do? Marry some rich man, as Chambers had suggested, and bring herself back to the station she had stood upon before her father died? He could force himself to think of such a thing calmly, now, when he could no longer offer her his stained name. Yet she had worn gladness in her eyes, that day when he had seen her last. Had she loved him then? Did she love him now? or was he blotted out of her thoughts? It gave him a thrill, even then, to think that if she forgot him she must forget him wilfully; for he knew that she had loved him once. He knew that he could not have mistaken that gladness in her eyes.

He turned again to thinking — of Elsie, of his sister, as she sat, day after day, quiet as a statue, her hands folded in her lap, waiting for her father's least wish, and thinking of Jerome. Thinking of him, who wore the uniform of stripes, walked in a lock-step to his dinner, made chairs all day, and had the close-cut hair and the badge of the convict. It was something, at least, to have made a friend like that. Her clear, honest eyes looked at him in the darkness of his cell. The clock in the tower rang twice. He fell asleep.

CHAPTER XIV

He left the prison quietly, on a December day, lowering, but not cold. At his request no one came to Joliet to greet him.

" I should rather see you all again in Chicago, Will," he wrote. " I haven't much sentiment over it myself; but I think it would be pleasanter if we waited until the penitentiary was at least out of sight." So he came out alone, in the clothes he had worn the day of the trial. They hung a little loosely on him, for ten months of confinement had, in spite of his cheerfulness, told upon his physique. His hair was growing again, and besides, was covered by his cap. Those who saw him in the train, even though some of them had noticed that he got on at Joliet, thought probably, seeing the prison pallor and the clothes too loose, that he was recovering from some illness. Few men have carried away less taint of the prison in their eyes than Jerome Kent.

282

He leaned back in his corner of the seat and watched the backward-flying fields, damp and deserted. A woman, getting on at Broxton, came through the car hesitating; no double seat was free. At length she sat down by Jerome. She was neither young nor pretty, and yet his heart leaped for the first time since he had tasted freedom. If he was a leper, at least he did not show it in his face. He wondered what the woman would do, should he lean over and say, " Madam, I am a convict two hours out of prison." The train boy came yelling down the aisle with the Chicago papers of the day. Jerome stared out of the window, but the woman, fumbling in her purse, bought a paper — the *Eye,* with flaring headlines about nothing. One of them caught Jerome's eye. " Notorious Convict Released To-day. Recalls the Wheeler-Northrop case of last February. History of the Crime." That he should thus be heralded, not allowed to slip quietly back into the city, he had not anticipated, and in the sickness of the discovery he was more than ever glad that none of his friends were there to share the pain.

Chambers met him at the station.

" Hello, Jerome."

" Hello, Will! " They shook hands.

" Mary didn't come down," said Chambers.
" She thought maybe you'd rather see me
alone a minute. It's good to have you back,
Jerry."

" It's better to be here, old man."

Chambers led the way out of the station.
" I see the cars are running on the elevated,
aren't they? I didn't know that."

" Four months," agreed Chambers, briefly.

" Where are we going, Will? "

" Up to my house, of course. Aren't you
even coming to dinner with us, you beggar?
Don't you remember once when you doomed
me to live in a boarding house all my days, because housekeeping cost too much? *I'll* show
you a house in a few minutes, and you'll be
sorry when you see it you haven't taken Solomon's advice."

Jerome smiled. " Do you still insist it was
Solomon? You are — too good to me, Will."

" Hell! " replied Chambers. " I've stopped
swearing, to please Mary," he apologized; " but
you would make St. Francis cuss."

They talked little, threading dismal, busy

streets toward the northeast. At length they reached their car; after that the journey was easy. "Here we are!" announced Chambers at length, when they arrived at a cross street, running into Lincoln Park. "And here's the flat, and here's Mary!"

There she was indeed, not quite so frail (disgracefully fat, Chambers declared her to be), just as much afraid of Jerome as she had been the first time they met, but very glad to see him. When they had shaken hands, Chambers put an arm on Jerome's shoulder. "Come along, Jerry," he said. "I want to show you the house." He led him down a tiny hallway. "That was the parlour you were in," he declared; "that's Mary's room and mine. Here's the dining room — plenty big enough for eight, if they are all good friends." He threw open a door. "And here," he said, with a trace of excitement in his voice, "is your room, Jerry."

Kent looked around. His trunk was in one corner, his pictures were upon the wall; the desk chair that had been his father's stood beside the table, and his books lay upon it. There were papers scattered loosely on the blotting-pad, under his lamp. "You stepped out for a minute," Chambers cried, "but you've come back now, old boy."

Jerome said nothing. Chambers was disappointed. "Don't you like it, old man?"

"Ah, God, Will! I can never make it up to you."

"It wasn't my idea, it was Mary's." Chambers volubly defended himself from any charge of kindness. "At least we both thought we shouldn't care for the flat so much unless there was a place for you in it; and then Mary said we ought to keep the room ready so that you could come in at any time; so of course we did. And now let's go out to dinner. It's all right, Marykins," he cried when he saw his wife, "he likes it."

They, Chambers and his wife — did all the talking at dinner; perhaps it was the young reporter alone who did it all. He conveyed the news in spurts, interspersed with praises of his wife's housewifery; of their maid, undoubtedly the best in the city; of the small woolly black-and-white pup which rolled in an imbecile fashion about the floor, and which Chambers declared undoubtedly of pure-bred

Anglo-Saxon mastiff blood; of their wedding gifts — " one due from you, my boy, and don't you believe we'll let you off; we've got our eye on a neat little thing in mahogany pianos that's just what the flat needs," — and finally on the flat itself, which in spite of the patent fact that there were seven others in the same building of precisely the same size, shape, and finish, was declared by its owner, without fear of contradiction, to be the most convenient, comfortable, complete, and altogether beautiful set of apartments in the city of Chicago. " Too big for two, just big enough for three, and a Paradise for four," he finished, whereat his little wife blushed deeply.

" Oh, by the way, Jerry," he said, in one of the infrequent moments when he could get away from talk upon their belongings — " did you know they say old Wheeler's daughter is engaged to — whom do you think? Old man Cahill's youngest, Billy Cahill. You know Billy Cahill? He had a cocktail named for him when he was nineteen, but I think he's steadied since, and they say he's the flower of the flock now. It's funny when you come to think of it, for when Wheeler was alive Cahill would go round the block to knock on him, they said. You know they were in the Union Savings together for a long while, but Wheeler pulled out a year before he died. I reckon it's a good thing for the bank he did. Well, Cahill has money to burn, of course, and Billy I guess can still get up in the morning and light the fire; so the Wheelers are provided for. But the engagement knocks out the last chance of those colleges getting the fifty thousand *pro rata*. Old man Cahill has millions; but he can see a dollar at a hundred yards, and he won't let fifty thousand lie out in the rain until it gets rusty."

"When is she to be married?" asked Jerome.

Chambers shook his head. "Do you know, Jerry, Billy didn't tell me the last time I dined there!" he remarked humorously. "But I reckon all they're waiting for is the year to be up since the old man went to be boss in — "

"Will!" cried his wife.

"Calvary," finished Will.

So it was all over, thought Jerome. She was engaged to be married. He took it very quietly. One does not know how to express the change in his feelings toward her, as the days slipped by, except in one way — by writing the pronoun without the capital. In prison he had realized they two could never marry; and he wondered if he had really ever, even before that, had any hope that he might call her his before all the world. As he looked back, he did not believe that he had. He had dreamed at whiles; perhaps that was all. Even the dreams had faded when fate drove him to his ruin. He could not bring himself to think what sort of a man this Cahill was, whom she was to marry; but he wished her, in his heart, happiness in her life. Not much of late had been hers, he knew, and he wondered whether when she met the man to whom she was engaged, she wore gladness in her eyes.

He went to see Elsie the next day, as she had insisted that he should do, and when he would have shaken hands, she kissed him. " Welcome back, Jerome," she said. Her voice was more cheerful and her eyes were brighter, he thought, than he had ever seen them; and there was colour in her cheeks. She was no more marble, but a girl who was alive. " You are to come directly up and see papa," she told

U

him. "He has been so impatient for the last few days that if I keep you here one single minute he will be running down." So she took him up to Northrop's sitting room.

"He is quite well now?" Jerome asked in the hallway.

"Quite, quite well. He never will be very strong, but then he never was. He has retired from the *Eagle,* you know. He talks of going back to the country and starting a weekly there, but he never will. Mamma cries at the mere mention of it!" she laughed.

Northrop held his hand a long time. He rose from his chair from the window, which was no longer locked; but Jerome made him sit down again. Northrop was thin, of course, but not with the skeleton-like deathly frailty that he had showed a year ago. His blue eyes under the blue-veined lids and the white hair were clear and straightforward, not shifting about the room. As his daughter said, he was quite well. Indeed, of the two Jerome was the paler. Jerome no longer wore the suit in which he had gone to prison, but these clothes, like the others, fitted him loosely, showing how much he had lost in weight.

" Life begins now in earnest for me," Northrop said at last. " It is worth while to work
in the sun, when the twilight is like this. Do
you know of any one who desires a first-class
certificated nurse, my boy? Mine is out of a
situation now, but I will give her the highest
recommendations." He glanced at Elsie.

" I shall not leave," she answered, " until I
get my wages."

" You see," Northrop complained, " I cannot get rid of her, for she knows I can't pay
her."

He spoke of Wheeler's death without hesitation. " He was a strong man — a terribly
strong man," he said. " I never could have
beaten him; he had to beat himself. While I
have been sitting here in the past year, I have
wondered sometimes whether I did him justice;
whether I really cared so much about the city,
or if a great deal of my feeling was only simple
hate. I am afraid a great deal of it was, and
that I showed it plainly. There is no more of
it left in me now. I wish, before he died, we
might have shaken hands. His will was very
touching, they say. He made it a kind of
declaration of principles. It was so confident

and bold and direct — and then everything had crumbled!"

He changed the subject. "Do you know," he went on, "that my wife has come round about the hawthorn? She has let me plant it even in the grounds here; and next summer I can see it from this window. Ah, when your family believe you ill, my boy, they put a terrible club in your hands, a terrible club!"

"He does not know," Elsie told Jerome afterward, "what happened at the trial. He does not remember the trial at all, and has no idea he was there. He knows that he was — ill — but he thinks he was taken ill earlier."

"I am glad of that."

When they had talked for a while of little things, came a pause — the pause they had both been fearing. Jerome ended it.

"Do you ever see — her, Elsie?"

She nodded. "But very seldom. I go out so little, and so does she. But now and then I meet her."

"Is she happy?"

"Happy?"

"In her engagement?" Elsie looked her surprise, and he went on hurriedly. "Will —

Mr. Chambers — told me of it. It was a bit soon, Elsie." A trace of bitterness showed in his voice.

" But is it true? " she questioned. " You are sure it is true? "

Up to the moment no doubt had come into his mind. He had accepted the situation, sorrowfully, but once and for all. Now the doubt came suddenly, powerfully, with a strange and disquieting pleasure. Then he shook his head.

" So Will says."

But Elsie was unconvinced. " I have heard the talk," she answered slowly, " and — yes, I have thought it might be so. But shouldn't you wait for the announcement before you let yourself believe? "

Again the sweetness of the doubt enveloped him; and again the reaction followed. Was the old battle to be fought again, with his destiny — the inevitable surrender bitterly to be remade? He and Ethel Wheeler were thrust apart. This he knew; the sorrow and the first sharp shock of pain were past. Behold, they leaped to life again at the first faint sound of a call.

"I suppose it is true.   And even if it is not — "

"Even then?"

He took Elsie's hand and spoke, holding it, as if the warm touch strengthened him. "Does it seem to you disloyalty, if I will not put that 'even then' to myself? Oh, Elsie, I have been trying so long to bear this shock; and when it came, and I found that I *could* bear it; that perhaps my life was not all ended yet; that somewhere remained a place for me, and a work, and even a forgetfulness — when I᾽ found that, Elsie, I was really happy. Must I give that up, too, now? *Is* my life ended?"

She listened, understanding, a great eagerness in her eyes.

"Ended? It is just begun."

But he followed on his own thoughts. "Then when you suggest, even ever so faintly, that she is *not* bound; that she is waiting; do you know what comes in my heart? All my dead hopes are alive again; all my struggles for resignation are to be gone through with once more. Is my life worth living, so? I cannot have what I desire. I gave it up; I tried to kill my longing. Must I be forever

giving it up and wanting it again? Must I
beat myself forever against this same wall?
Am I never to leave prison?" He still held
her hand, but he had forgotten he was speaking to her, and was living over alone in his
thoughts the long nights of his cell. "Oh,
Elsie, tell me — am I to dare to hope?"

"Are you afraid to have me speak openly,
Jerome?" Elsie's voice had lost the brightness, and came calm, evenly modulated, as she
had used to speak when he first knew her. The
hand he held fluttered a little, but was not with-
drawn.

"Go on, please," he asked her.

"Have you fought it out with yourself,
then, so often?" she questioned. "Have you
wondered if you could bury the past; if you
and she could remember — and forget? Have
you done this?"

He nodded, watching her straightforward
eyes.

"And then — what have you decided?"

"As you know," he answered heavily.

"Oh," she broke out, "it is bitter, it is cruel,
to torment you, to torment us both, on this day
when we should be happy. But what can I

do? I know you are hoping now; I know you are wondering if I, too, and the world, and she, think as you do. What can I do? What can I say? I must be honest, dear, dear Jerome, — " and then she stopped. " I think — I think you ought to forget about her, Jerome."

His clasp on her hands tightened till her fingers paled, and then he loosed her.

" Thank you, Elsie," he said. " You are a good friend to me."

" Yes," she answered, with a curious, strained look in her clear eyes. " Yes, Jerome, I think I am."

When he had left her she went up to her room and stared into her glass. At length she was satisfied. " No, he did not know," she thought. She had dealt honestly with him. Suppose he had guessed what her honesty cost? Suppose he knew that she — that she — suppose he wondered if anything lay behind her honesty beside friendship? Suppose he fancied she had spoken as she did, intimated that his dead hopes might not be raised again, because — she wanted him for herself? She shuddered. The fear that he would fancy that had been a knife in her heart. Almost she had betrayed her friendship, let him cherish his false hopes again, just to save her own self from that fear. But she had been true. She *had* been a good friend to him. He was humility itself, and would never guess; she was calmness itself, and he would never guess. " No," she whispered pitifully, " he will never know." And she tried to smile at the face that had been so calm. Then she went once more to her father.

Jerome began work on the following day. Northrop's influence secured him a position as an agent for an Eastern periodical, in which his ability to read and criticise and estimate served him in good stead, and which still gave him time for his own work. The old man told him about the place hesitatingly. " It's hardly what I should like to get you, my boy; but — a little later — Meanwhile this will serve." Jerome accepted it as simply as it was offered.

One of the first things he did was to write a note to Judge Hetheridge, asking permission to call. " Certainly," Hetheridge answered. And when Jerome had been in Chicago about a

week, he went over one evening and told the
Judge his story.

"I was punished for what I did, and I do
not complain," he said, "but I should like you
to know exactly my crime."

Hetheridge shook hands when he went away.
"I hope you will come again," he said heartily.
"I believe every word you say. Come again,
my boy, come again, but don't come in — " the
old joke, his favourite among them all, died
upon his lips. But Jerome smiled.

"No, Judge Hetheridge," he answered, "I
won't come any more — in business hours."

The days went on. He spent Christmas with
the Chambers's and New Year's Day with the
Northrops. He was busy, — busy with his
work, busy with his book, which he took up
again, laughed to see how crude it was, tossed
aside, picked up again, — and was lost.
Mother-love, they say! If one desires a symbol
of affection, why not take the love of the young
writer for his first book? He was astounded
first, then glad, to see how small an impression
his life had made upon the tremendous city.
Daily contact with men was nothing like so
difficult and unpleasant as he had feared. They

might talk, occasionally, behind his back; but few seemed to know, fewer still to care, that he had been a convict. When his book was published, it came out under an assumed name — John Scannell — for he desired to avoid the public recall of his imprisonment. When the first copies came into his hands, he took one to Northrop. The old man complimented him pleasantly. Elsie was happy; Chambers wildly enthusiastic. Yet Jerome felt something lacking in his heart — not from them, but in his own feelings. He waited some days; and then, yielding at last to his impulse, he sealed up a copy himself, addressed it, sent it away. And in a few days more there came an answer.

The handwriting he knew at once, though only one line of it he had ever seen. He read the little note.

" Thank you. I remember that I knew the book when few did, and I am proud. I am sure that it is the beginning of a career." That was all. Nor was the letter signed.

Jerome knew all that was to be known of Ethel Wheeler. She lived quietly with her mother; they seldom went out. The wreck of the old colossal fortune, so little that even the colleges had no heart to snatch it, was enough for the two women. The rumoured engagement to Cahill was long since denied; others had sprung up and been denied in turn. Ethel Wheeler was still Ethel Wheeler. And so he wrote to her, at length, and begged that he might call. She answered at once. She should be very glad to see him.

A trifle of the old constraint with which they had first met, lay upon them now. He had been thinking of her for three years, without a sight of her face. When he saw it he knew that his memory had not played him false. She was quieter; her eyes danced less; but the old strong firm curves were there, the sunshiny hair was unsubdued as ever, the sweetness and the beauty were the same. Looking at her, his first thought was of wonderment and humility.

They talked of his book, and of his plans. They were alone, for her mother had angrily declined to come down. They broke off into little pauses, which they hastened to fill up. He could not say what he wished; indeed, he did not know what he wished to say. And presently it was time for him to go.

"When may I come again?" he asked her awkwardly. He was standing; his shoulders had broadened out again, and his strong figure seemed oddly unauthorlike. She looked at him without rising.

"Do you think, Mr. Kent, that you had better come again?"

He caught his breath; the waters which had rolled back, came flooding over him once more. He looked at her stupidly. Then she rose.

"Do you think," she continued, "it is easy for me to say that? Do you think I should not like you for a friend? That I have forgotten we were friends once? No; we have not forgotten. So — that is why, Mr. Kent."

The revulsion left him weak as water. He put his hand upon a chair. Suddenly, as they had done before, his dead hopes, his old longings, rose and marched before his eyes. He willed them away, but they would not go. He looked, and he knew that they had never been dead. They had deceived him so long, but it was all deception. His resignation was gone to the winds. His knowledge of the world, his resolution, his command of self, — where were they? One thing he knew — he loved, as he had loved before, and would still continue to love, this girl, this jewel of the days. She had loved him once; did she love him still? She must, she should, she did!

"Oh, Ethel, Ethel, Ethel!" His heart was in the name.

"Hush, hush!" she answered. The curves of her face set. She grew older before his eyes. "Oh, hush, please, please!"

But he would not be stopped, as years before he had refused to be. He told her, in a torrent, of his thoughts, his longings, and his love; his resignation, and his hopes, and then his love again. He came back to that always, clung to it, would not think of anything but that, nor have her think of anything, but meant to sweep her away. She listened, with her eyes down, bending a little forward, until he paused. Then she said, —

"And my mother, Mr. Kent?"

It was as if she had whispered "Listen!" They stood looking at one another. The glow was still upon his face, his eyes still flashed, his shoulders squared, and as if that mother had heard, her voice, shrill, nervous, tired, came down the staircase.

"Ethel!"

"Yes, mother."

"I want you."

"Yes, mother. In just a moment." She turned to Jerome and flung out her hands. "Don't you see? Oh, don't you see? It is not only she who stands between us; it is my father, and my past. We cannot remember a little and forget the rest. We cannot be children any more, and just pretend. Oh!" she went on, "I have prayed, sometimes, Mr. Kent, that this might never happen, and then I have wondered if perhaps it were not better to have it happen after all. I have wanted to tell you that I am proud of you; that I have always been proud of you; that I believe in you. You have your life to live, and your work to do. Once — I *will* tell you — I fancied I might perhaps share them with you, help you a little, maybe. But that is over. Go to your work; succeed, succeed! I know you will. I shall not tell you to forget me, and I shall not forget you. I am your friend. But you must not see me. It is a puzzle. God knows why He gave it to us. I may have solved it all wrong. But this is my answer to it. I am my mother's daughter — and my father's."

"Ethel!" came the voice again.

"Good-by," she said hurriedly.

"Good-by," he answered, not dully now, but with his head up, and his shoulders firm again. The old humility was upon him, with the old heart-ache. Heart-ache! who was he in the presence of this magnificent girl, so sure, so strong, so fine? At the least, if it was hard for him, he could make it easier for her. "Good-by," he answered. "I can understand." He went away. And when he had closed the door, she sat down, as one who could not trust herself to stand, and the tears filled her eyes, and she bowed her head upon her arms — she, who had been made for gladness and for joy.

"Ethel!" called her mother, querulously, for the third time.

"Yes, dear," she answered, moving up.

"I saw — Miss Wheeler to-day," Jerome told Elsie that evening. She looked at him, waiting. But he stared silently into the fire, thinking better of his impulse. She rose, and going to the piano, began to sing softly. At length she ceased.

"I must go up to my work," he said abruptly.

"Is the new story getting on?"

"The new one? Yes; yes." He laughed cynically. "And the old one — is finished. Good night, Elsie."

She was more than vaguely troubled, and she strove to detain him. "What shall you call it, Jerome?"

He looked down at her, and saw the pity in her face, and the momentary cynicism was rent from him with a cry.

"The sins of the fathers, Elsie, the sins of the fathers!" The heroism was quite gone out of him; he was only a boy whose heart was broken, and he dropped upon his knees beside her and buried his head in her lap; and she smoothed his hair.

x

www.ingramcontent.com/pod-product-compliance
Lightning Source LLC
Chambersburg PA
CBHW030342020726
47493CB00003B/649

*9 7 8 1 4 3 4 4 0 7 0 2 3 *